ONE
TWO
KILL
A
FEW

A CASEY FREMONT MYSTERY

ONE TWO KILL A FEW

A CASEY FREMONT MYSTERY

JOHN ACHOR

Acacia Imprints

ELKHORN, NEBRASKA

Description: fiction, mystery, female, amateur sleuth

This is a work of fiction. Names, characters, places and incidents are either products of author's imagination or are used fictitiously. Any resemblance to actions or persons, living or dead, events or locales is entirely coincidental.

Paperback ISBN: 978-1-949601-01-5

Kindle ISBN: 978-1-949601-02-2

Library of Congress Copyright Number: 2018953454

Cataloging in Publication Data on file with Publisher.

ACACIA IMPRINTS

John Achor

Email: john@johnachor.com

Author's Links:

BLOG: http://www.johnachor.wordpress.com/

FACEBOOK: http://www.facebook.com/jachor1

TWITTER: twitter.com/caseyfremont

WEB SITE: www.johnachor.com

3rd Edition, 2018

10 9 8 7 6 5 4 3 2 1

READER REVIEWS ABOUT
ONE, TWO – KILL A FEW

My three girls gave me a Kindle a few days before I got your e-mail. Your book was my first purchase. *One, Two – Kill a Few* is great! I mean it!! It is an attention grabbing, don't want to put it down kind of book.

GLYNDA B

Read your mystery, *One, Two – Kill a Few*, and enjoyed it very much. I've been a mystery fan for 50 years and read just about every Sherlock Holmes story from Arthur Conan Doyle and Hercule Piorot/Miss Marple stories by Agatha Christie. Most of Agatha's paperbacks were read multiple times and I finally donated 2 plastic bags of them to my local library. Since all of those stories were set in the distant past and mostly in England I wasn't sure how I would respond to a modern mystery set in Little Rock.

Bottom line - I found your book not only a refreshing change from the aforementioned scenarios but a very enjoyable and interesting read.

ROBERT B

John Achor draws the audience into the mystery immediately with "raining bodies." The reader's curiosity is hooked as the story progresses with the addition of friends to help solve the mystery. A growing romance with the police detective holds the reader's attention as the killers are tracked through the evolving story. I enjoyed every page and would recommend it to all who read mysteries. I'm looking forward to more Casey Fremont books. Thank you, Mr. Achor.

RITA D

OTHER BOOKS BY JOHN ACHOR

Casey Fremont mysteries
One, Two – Kill A Few
Three, Four – Kill Some More
Five, Six – Deadly Mix

Alex Hilliard thrillers
Assault on the Presidency

DEDICATION

To my wife Pat for her understanding and patience.

ACKNOWLEDGMENTS

My profound thanks go to our three children for editorial assistance, suggestions, and who always give me inspiration and encouragement. Any number of coffee house and book store managers who didn't run me out but allowed me to linger over a cup of coffee as I wrote including bagel shops and various casinos which provide numerous places for an author to sit and write while his wife beats up their slot machines.

My thanks also go to a Hot Springs critique group: Fred Boling, Elizabeth Foster, Leon Hardin, Pug Jones, Margaret Morrell, Mary Ann Robertson, Bill White and Madelyn Young (I feel I've missed someone and for that I apologize). This group shared their time, knowledge and expertise providing me with more assistance than an author could expect. If there are any errors in this work, they are mine. If I strayed from the straight and narrow, hopefully it was due to writer's license or fictionalization and not pure error.

1

MY NAME'S CASEY FREMONT. LOTS OF FOLKS shorten my nickname even further, to KC. I used to go by those initials, but got tired of answering the question, "Does KC stand for somethin'?" Well of course it stands for something, Dimbulb. I even tried "Ms. Fremont," but that made me sound too old. My mother wasn't frightened by the Initial Imps, though something must have scared her. I've never been able to get her to tell me where she came up with Acacia, which is the long version of Casey.

* * *

This morning started out so well, I thought I was on a roll. I hoped the rest of the day would be as great. It wasn't, but how could I know it would be raining bodies before noon.

I put on one of my best business suits. It's a dark, dark gray pin stripe. The jacket is double-breasted and the slit skirt doesn't quite make it down to mid-thigh. I've never been turned down during an interview, but it never hurts to flash a bit of leg at a male interviewer. It's fun to watch where their eyes wander during the discussion. A lot of men have trouble looking a woman in the eye. More often they are gazing at the assets a good bit south of the face.

I was heading for Little Rock's Midtown Atrium Towers Building, a new expanse of glass and steel in the downtown area. In keeping with the new architecture, an atrium reaches to the top between two buildings. I would be talking to a Wayne Harmon at Cyber-Technology, a computer and internet consulting firm.

At quarter past nine, fifteen minutes before my appointment, I walked through the huge glass doors, which opened for me with an automatic whoosh. The main floor entrance was through a curved glass wall going up all twelve floors. A similar wall of glass faced me from the rear of the lobby and the sign over the far doorway read: Parking Garage. I glanced around the lobby at the large planter areas replete with foliage and flowers. There were even a couple of imported palm trees; far from native to Arkansas. Buildings stretched upward to my left and to my right. The structure smelled like a new building. The faint but pungent aroma left from new carpet glued to the floor drifted past me. I checked the directory and learned Cyber-Technology was in Tower B, the one on the right.

The elevators were glass and brass clinging to the walls of the atrium. It would be an interesting ride—I'm not afraid of heights, but I don't like looking straight down at nothing between me and a sudden stop at the bottom. I was almost across the lobby when I heard the shout from behind me.

"Damn, look out!"

The last word was shouted in my ear as something slammed into my back. I hit the polished marble floor with a thud knocking most of the air out of my lungs. Then a crushing weight on my back forced the rest of the air to be expelled. I was gasping for breath. I heard a sickening thud, and a couple of seconds later there was another sound. More of a plop than a thud.

"Are you okay, lady?" said the man lying on my back.

"I will be as soon as you get the hell off me."

"I'm sorry." He rolled away, struggled to his feet and offered his hand.

With effort, I managed a sitting position, slapped his hand aside and tugged at my skirt. "What the hell was that all about?" I used my most annoyed voice and scowl.

"The guy took a header off an atrium balcony. He damn near fell on top of you."

I looked over my shoulder and saw it. It…was a body, sprawled in a grotesque position, about six feet from me. The eyes were open, but they saw nothing. One leg and one arm lay at angles normal limbs are unable to assume. Blood oozed from a flat spot on his head, from his mouth and from the ear turned toward me. The blood spread out on the light-colored marble and seeped into the expansion joints.

That'll be a bitch to clean up, I thought. I shook my head in disbelief at myself; strange, the thoughts that run through a mind under stress.

"I've got to get upstairs," I said. "I've got an interview."

"Better stay here. I think the cops will want to talk to you," my Good Samaritan said.

"Why me? I didn't see anything."

"You are still a witness." He extended his hand again. This time I took it and let him pull me to my feet. Building security was already milling around the lobby, and I could hear sirens approaching outside.

2

HOW DID I GET HERE THIS MORNING? I SUPPOSE I should bring you up to date. Yesterday morning started out so well—I was thinking: I got it made. All my bills covered for another month. Today would clinch the fact there was more money than month left. I pulled on a pair of baggy, gray sweatpants, an old Liz Claiborne T-shirt, and took the elevator to the ground floor of my condo building to get the mail. Good old Ted the Postman was taking his usual sweet time sorting letters. I sat on a couch, on the far side of the lobby, and watched and waited. Once upon a time, I stood near the boxes with the hope it would expedite the sorting process. Didn't work. Ted had time to doze each time his hand dipped into the huge leather pouch for another batch. Slow, rhythmic—the movement resembled an ancient and long forgotten martial arts sequence of exercises. I learned to hover at a discreet distance. Lurking nearer seemed to slow the process beyond anything bearable.

Fifteen minutes of my life later, ritual complete, Ted swung the hinged cover shut and locked it. That was his cue to us waiters—I was joined by three other hopefuls during the wait—the mail now resided in its proper bin and was available for retrieval. I covered the distance to the boxes with as much speed as I could while maintaining a bit of decorum. My sneakers squeaked on the marble floor and drew stares from Ted and the other denizens of my building.

"I forgot. It's Mother's Day," Ted said, looking at me.

I pulled up short of the boxes, eyebrows raised. "What?"

"Over in the projects, they call it Mother's Day. The day the welfare checks come."

I screwed on my most indignant scowl and said, "It's not welfare. It's due-fare."

"What?" It was Ted's turn.

"I put in almost fifteen years with that asshole. Half of the time I was supporting him. Now the fare is due me—it's alimony. In his case, you could call it: the screwin' he's getting for the screwin' around he did."

Two additional pairs of eyebrows slid up their owners' foreheads and I heard a gasp of air escape from each of the ladies. This time it was from my co-waiters, standing in front of their own mailboxes. Two of the three appeared to be on the verge of apoplexy, even their ears turned red.

Kenley Longstreet, a first-name, same-floor, nod-of-the-head type neighbor, took it in stride. "The swine," he said. "I can't imagine anyone treating you in such a manner, Casey."

I reached down and tugged the legs of my sweats up to my calves.

"What, dear lady," Kenley said, the tone still dripping honey, "causes such a reaction?"

"It's getting deep around here, and I wanta be ready to wade through ankle deep bullshit." I grinned and Kenley returned a wink.

Two mailbox doors slammed in unison behind me. I turned in time to see Mrs. Abigail Rosewood, from the third floor, purse her lips and give Mrs. Martha Farley, who lives one floor above me, a terse head shake. The color on both their faces matured to a deeper shade of crimson and spread downward, causing already bulging tendons to appear more obvious. They stomped toward the bank of elevators and I saw Kenley's features light up like a morning glory opening and turning its face to the sun.

"Well spoken, Casey. I apologize for the earlier turn of phrase, and I did so enjoy how your words affected the Brewster sisters," he said.

He must have noticed my confused expression.

"Oh, I know their last names are different, but Abby and Martha Brewster…the two old busy-body sisters who poisoned their gentlemen callers in—*Arsenic and Old Lace*—the movie. I'm certain you must remember the movie?"

I nodded and went back to my reason-for-being this morning. I unlocked my box and extracted the latest issue of Self and half-dozen envelopes. I tucked the magazine under my arm and shuffled through the letters. Must have missed it. I reshuffled the stack of envelopes one…by…one…and verified my first conclusion.

"Shit!" The word exploded from my mouth—louder than I intended—loud enough to jerk Kenley back out of the elevator.

He stood there holding the door open. "Is the asshole late again with the alimony check?" Kenley said. He's overheard enough of my rants to know about Jarvis and the alimony. I smiled at him and for the hundredth time, tried to guess his age—one of the "ever young" faces. I pegged him at sixty, though I knew I could be a decade off, either direction.

I nodded. "Yep, Jarvis Parnell Sheffield da Third, Esquire, has once again screwed the pooch. I'm certain he has fifty reasons for being late, but believe you me…he will pay." I got into the elevator car and rode up to the eighth floor with Kenley.

I shook my head and entered my condo. I fought off one of those moments of insecurity which plagued me more and more these days, and decided it was time to get in touch with my second favorite asshole—the one at TrueTemp.

* * *

An hour later I pushed open the door at True Temp. In reality, I shoved it so hard it slammed into a chair inside. Becca Rider was startled by my entrance and glanced up from her receptionist's desk. She gave me a nod and a shrug that said oh-it's-you-again and spoke into her headset, "TrueTemp, your full service temporary employment agency. How may I help you?"

I mouthed a "Hello" to Rebecca and took a seat. I knew she would get me in to see her boss as soon as she was off the phone. There was a young lady in the waiting room who could pass for a teenybopper. She looked about the age Jarvis, my ex, would chase around a desk. There was a bright expectant look in her eyes, but I could tell by her well-worn clothes she was in desperate need of a job. She'd be lucky to get into an interview, let alone survive one looking this bad. I assessed what I saw—she wasn't dirty, she needed a new dress, some grooming tips and in all probability, some interview skills.

There you go again, Casey, I thought. Ready to take on the rest of the world's woes. Settle for your own—you need a paycheck to get to the end of the month.

Becca finished her call by setting an appointment with the person on the other end of the phone. She pushed what must have been an intercom button, and spoke loud enough for me to hear. "Rutledge, Casey is out here in the waiting room. There seems to be a fire in her eye." Becca winked at me and continued, "I think you better see her right away."

Becca pumped her head up and down and jerked a thumb over her shoulder toward the office of TrueTemp owner, Rutledge Trueblood. I was familiar with the creep. In the days following my divorce, I signed on with his agency because I was in desperate need of money.

Jarvis the Rat, in his case it's the easiest way to spell lawyer, acted as his own counsel in our divorce and screwed it up in the worst way. The judge awarded me a large settlement as well as the hefty alimony commitment, which was due the first of each month. Jarvis the Rat remained true to character. Now he contested the lump sum figure and every month came up with new reasons why he was late with my alimony check. I learned his fervent prayer was that I would default on the condo mortgage and be thrown out on the sidewalk with few, if any, material belongings.

I said I was desperate, but not desperate enough to accept the care and concern offered—nay, thrust upon me—by Rutledge the Rutter. The second time I came to this agency, he invited me into his office. His big mistake was not closing the door. He put both his hands on my breasts and murmured how attractive I was. My response—I brought my right hand up between his legs and got a firm grasp on his family jewels. As my fingers curled around his privates, he relinquished his hold on me and let out a horrific howl.

Becca and another applicant stuck their heads into the office. I asked Rutledge to explain to them what he was up to. He declined and my grip tightened.

"I - I - I was…fondling…Casey's breasts," he said. The words were interspersed between rasping gulps for air.

I presented my demands: he was to be available to me whenever I called, he would expend two hundred percent on my behalf, find me a paycheck within twenty-four hours of my call, and protect both my witnesses, Becca and the applicant. In return I would not sue for sexual harassment or do what he feared the most—I would not tell his wife and the newspapers.

My final words to him were, "Rutledge, if I even hear you are forcing yourself on somebody else, I swear by all that's holy, I'll see you rot in hell…and on the front page." With Becca as my inside operative, we've managed to keep ol' Rutledge more than an arm's length from all his female clients.

Becca and the applicant would both participate in my good fortune. Since then, all I need to do is let Rutledge know I need money and I've got a position by the following day.

Again today, I saw the fear of retribution on his face, and within thirty minutes I was on my way out of the TrueTemp agency. The note in my purse contained a name, address and an interview time for the following morning.

3

I WAS STILL STARING AT THE DEAD BODY, WHEN MY stomach did a flip-flop and my benefactor told me his name was Gene Morse. He looked like he wanted to talk, but we both could see the doorman pointing at us and the police officers moving our direction.

"Here is my card. Do you have one?" he said. When I shook my head, he added, "Well, if you work around here, give me a call. Maybe we can have lunch…or something."

The day's looking up, I thought. Good-looking blond making a pass at me. Even with bodies dropping around us, the place can't be all bad.

I looked at the policeman who approached us. He introduced himself. "What should I call you, Detective Sergeant Epstein?" I said.

"Detective will be fine, ma'am. I understand you saw the deceased fall to his death."

Gene excused himself and moved back toward the elevators.

"Well, not exactly." I recounted my experience from the time I entered the building until I was shoved and heard the man hit the floor. "What was his name?"

"I'm afraid we can't release that information yet. May I have your full name and address…and phone number?"

I rattled off my name, my initials and the story about using my initials rather than my first name. Whoa, Casey, I thought. Why the rambling discourse about the name? I took a closer look at Detective Epstein and realized why. Dennis—I wormed his first name out of him while babbling about initials—Dennis was a hunk. I figured him about six feet tall. Easy deduction—the two-inch heels I was wearing that day put me at five-ten and he was at least a couple of inches above me. He was good looking in a rugged sort of way—the black, wavy hair and green eyes helped—and not married. I hoped the lack of a ring on the left hand spelled single. I also hoped my attentiveness wasn't as obvious as it seemed to me.

"Can you think of anything else, Ms. Fremont?"

"No, and I need to get going. I have a job interview up on the ninth floor." He nodded, so I added, "If you'll give me your card, I'll call you if I remember anything else."

He smiled. "That's supposed to be my line."

He held the business card between the first two fingers as he offered it to me. As I reached for it, he said, "Since I have your home number, perhaps I could call you…to see if you've remembered anything else."

"That would be nice." Oh, Lord, Casey—how inane. I snatched the extended card and hurried toward the elevators.

Inside the glass enclosure, I punched the "9" button. I saw a small note taped across the buttons for the tenth, eleventh and twelfth floors. It read: No Admittance - Under Construction. I thought about the lobby. The dead guy bleeding all over the floor wasn't pleasant, but…I thought, I'm the proud possessor of two business cards, from two attractive men—both apparently interested in me. The day's getting better and better.

The elevator chimed and the doors slid open without a sound. The double glass doors in front of me displayed large, stylized and linked letters, C-T embossed on both. I didn't see any signs pointing to any other businesses. It looked like Cyber-Technology occupied the whole floor.

"I have…had a nine-thirty appointment with Mr. Wayne Harmon," I told the woman behind the reception desk. The nameplate read: Cheryl Kennedy. I eyeballed her and tried to assess my chances of getting into the interview—a half-hour late.

"Yeah," she said. The word was sandwiched between noises as she popped her chewing gum. "Mr. Harmon's been wondering…" Snap. "where…" Snap. "you been."

I put on my most pathetic face and ran through the lobby story, including all the bloody details, in under a minute.

"Geez," Cheryl said. She leaped to her feet, moved ten feet down the hall and flung open an office door. "Mr. Harmon. The lady you been waiting for is here. And, you won't believe why she's late!"

I could hear Cheryl as she related my story—almost verbatim—beginning with, "There's a dead guy bleeding all over the lobby."

The story got me past the half-hour late problem. My resume and a short skirt got me past Wayne's questions. By this time we were on a first-name basis.

Harmon sat behind a huge glass-top desk. He said, "I'm impressed with your credentials."

I couldn't be sure if he was staring down at my resume on the glass desktop, or through the glass at my crossed legs.

Whichever it was, he said, "Can you start first thing tomorrow?" When I nodded, he added, "See Cheryl. She'll have any paperwork you need to fill out, and she can introduce you around the office. Complete the forms this morning, and you can hit the ground running tomorrow." He looked at his watch. "Let's assume you arrived on time. That puts you on the temp agency's payroll since nine-thirty today. Go on home as soon as you finish the paperwork and we'll assume you put in a full day."

I thanked Wayne, shook his hand and located Cheryl. I finished the usual ream of employment forms in twenty minutes. Working temp jobs taught me to have all the details ready, beforehand. No racking the brain for the job before the last one… having the information with me, I could copy data onto the forms with little effort. I finished and went back to Cheryl's desk. "The bosses are all computer nerds. I'll introduce you," she said.

Besides the owner, Wayne Harmon who interviewed me, there were three others she referred to as bosses. One by one, she dragged me to their offices. The first one looked like the back room at a small computer store. A workbench covered two walls and was littered with computer parts and repair equipment. The man sitting on a high stool at the bench paid scant attention to us, but did acknowledge our presence when Cheryl called his name. "Barry…Barry. This is Casey Fremont. She'll be filling in for Celia. Casey, this is Barry Peterson."

He twisted his head far enough to see me, waved and grunted something unintelligible.

I muttered a greeting as Cheryl pulled me away. I received similar welcomes in the other two offices Cheryl led me to. I began to think these people were all cold. Then it dawned on me. Computer geeks. No doubt good at what they do but lacking in the social graces and the ability to make friends.

Barry was their hardware man. Next I met the software wizard, Winston Eberheart. Another rumpled one. He sat at a small desk in front of a credenza holding three computers. Rumpled was too weak a word. One sleeve of his white shirt was rolled up past the elbow. The other was still buttoned at the cuff. His sport coat, which hung askew on a coat rack, looked almost like it was being used as a dust cloth. One sleeve and the whole side of his jacket were covered with a white, chalky substance. His aftershave hung in the air and threatened to envelop me. I couldn't place the brand, but I was sure it bore one of those macho names—like Brutus, or Stetson.

I learned their security guru was Ross Worthington. He was a tad neater than the others, but not much. His choice of clothing and colors bordered on the bizarre. I was reminded of an old joke about some high school whose colors were pomegranate and puce. He also mixed a plaid tie and checkered dress shirt with his pin-striped suit. I surmised he was required to meet with clients on the outside and hoped those clients had a sense of humor. The decor of his office was dated. Among others, there was a poster warning "The Y2K Bug—The Millennium Monster" was looming around the corner. Since January the first, 2000 came and went five years ago with few problems for computers, I hoped Ross was more current with his security suggestions.

Even with the introductions, I was back in the lobby before eleven.

Gene Morse was still there and he started toward me. Dennis beat him. C'mon guys, I thought. Don't fight over little ol' me. On second thought, go ahead—fight. Gene moved away again, and I turned toward Dennis.

"What's the big grin all about?" Dennis said.

"Nothing, you had to be there."

Dennis did a subtle double-take and shook his head. "Something came up, and I'd like to ask you about it."

I wondered what more I could add to what I already told him.

"We found one of the victim's shoes several feet away from the body. Nearly missed it—it was in a planter…did you notice the missing shoe?"

I shook my head.

"Well, did you hear it land?"

I thought back to the time I came through the automatic doors into the atrium. I was walking toward the elevators when Gene slammed into my back. I was propelled forward and lost my balance and…then there was the sound of the man's body hitting the floor…and…there was a little plop. "Something hit something a second or two after the body hit the floor. It wasn't much of a noise—it could have been a shoe."

"You sure it was after the body hit?"

"Yeah. Why?" I put my hands on my hips and stared at Dennis.

"I've forgotten most of my physics courses, but seems to me the shoe should have hit before or at the same time as the body…"

His voice trailed off, as if he spilled too many of the beans already. "Is it important?" I said. His lips were pressed together and I knew I wasn't going to get anything further from him.

I started for the exit but stopped long enough to say, "Don't forget to check later to see if I've remembered anything else. You still have my number, don't you?"

There was a smile on his face as I left the building. There was a smile on my face as well.

4

THE MIDTOWN ATRIUM TOWERS BUILDING WAS A short distance from the river. I decided to walk and eat lunch at a small cafe I know in the River Market area. The weather was decent, so I ate my salad at an outdoor table. Anticipating a reasonable paycheck in a week or so, I left a healthy tip for the attractive young lady who served my meal.

It was one o'clock and Becca would be back at her desk at TrueTemp. The morning was exciting and I wanted to share the events with someone. She was a kindred spirit, a good listener and would enjoy the story.

A six-block walk to the garage where I parked earlier took twenty-five minutes. If I used my treadmill pace, I could have covered the distance in far less time. I chalked it up to the heels, gawking at people and window-shopping.

When I told Becca the morning was successful and exciting, she transferred the phones to the answering service and stood up. She headed for the break room and waved for me to follow. We were seated at the small table, each with a cup of steaming decaf and a box containing three donuts between us.

I mentioned my lunch and begged off on the contents of the box. Becca selected, it seemed an almost painful process to pick one, the plumpest donut in the box. She squeezed it until the jelly oozed from the filler hole in the side. She placed her tongue to the donut and licked it clean before she said, "I always get ten of these in each dozen. Rutledge hates them." She leaned back with a self-satisfied grin on her face. "So, give. What happened this morning?"

I began and reached the point where Gene knocked me down. I was about to describe the body—

"Whoa, girl. What did the guy look like? Date material?"

I described Gene Morse and skipped out of sequence to the part where he gave me his card and asked me to call him. Becca's eyebrows did a flick up her forehead a couple of times.

She didn't add anything, so I went on. When I described the thud, the twisted leg and all the blood, Becca's hand stopped in mid-air. The donut in her hand was about three inches from the open mouth waiting for the next bite. Jelly dripped over a finger and dropped onto the table.

"Holy, Mary, mother of God," she said.

That's about as religious as Becca gets. I covered the rest of the morning for her. When I mentioned Dennis, her eyebrows did the flicking number again. She posed a dozen questions about the dead guy: Who was he? Where did he work? Why did he take a header off a balcony?

"I asked the same questions," I said. "Couldn't get Detective Epstein to tell me anything."

"Detective? I thought you two were on a first-name basis."

I grinned and went on with the story. When I finished, we both sat back to contemplate the day's events. Becca pointed to the last donut. I shook my head and she plucked it from its resting place.

After a reasonable period of mourning for the empty box— about the time it took her to devour the last, lone jelly-filled—she leaned forward. "You remember that girl, Effie that was in here yesterday? That mousy one?"

I did. I also remembered thinking she was going to need help if she was going to get a job. I nodded.

"Well, I got her an interview for this morning. 'Bout five minutes into the scheduled interview time, I get a call. The guy says she doesn't present the proper appearance and I tell him to send her back here."

By this time, I was beginning to smell something fishy. And, it wasn't tuna salad.

"When Effie got here this morning," Becca said, "I could see what he meant. You 'member the character in that book, *Larceny and Old Lace* by that Tamar Myers? You know, the one who was a seamstress of dubious talent. Made all her own clothes and they was always fallin' apart?"

I remembered the story and what she was talking about. I cringed. The fishy smell turned into a prickly feeling, which was clawing its way up my back.

Rutledge Trueblood peered through the open door to the break room, a scowl on his face. "Becca, coffee," he said.

Becca jerked a thumb over her shoulder toward the pot. The Rutter growled a harrumph and disappeared back down the hall—without coffee.

"I get him his first cup in the morning," Becca said. "After that, he's on his own. He knows better." She fixed me with her eyes. "I gave her, Effie, a couple of dollars and sent her around the corner for some lunch. She'll be back in a few minutes…and…"

"And what? Why are you looking at me like you know something I don't?" She knows me too well. I knew there was a plan for Effie brewing, and the feeling up my back told me I would be involved in a most intimate and time consuming manner.

Becca was staring at me and I swear she was reading my mind.

"C'mon, Casey. It won't take much of your time."

She outlined the idea. All I needed to do was take Effie home with me, teach her how to dress and act, and help her get a job. Playing Professor Henry Higgins to this girl, Effie Tremayne, flashed through my mind. From the look on Becca's face, I could tell she was sure the hook was set. I hoped Effie would be as quick a study as Eliza Doolittle was.

"Why in the world are you so interested in this girl?" I said.

"She puts me in mind of a relative of mine and she comes from the same area over near Smackover."

"Someone you grew up with?"

"No. A second cousin twice removed or something like that. Used to see her every year at family reunions. A good girl who could use some help."

I figured my fate was sealed and didn't bother to argue any further.

When Effie returned, Becca escorted her to the break room where I was still sitting. I saw what Becca alluded to earlier. Effie wore a print dress—not a single seam enjoyed a match with the material's pattern. The hem on one side drooped due to poor stitching or the lack thereof. I'm lousy with needle, thread and sewing machines. I wouldn't be of any help in the homespun clothes department, but I know a trick or two. I also maintained an outstanding relationship with the lady who runs and owns Second Time Around.

"Effie, this here is Casey Fremont. She's gonna give you some help findin' a job."

Inside, I cringed. I plastered a smile on the outside and shook the hand Effie extended. Good. A firm handshake.

Effie said, "Thank you for the offer, but I need to go back home. I don't have enough money to rent a place to stay."

Becca leapt into the conversation. Good thing it was talk she was jumping into—because making a physical leap anywhere for a gal her size could be a gargantuan feat. She blurted out the fact there was a spare bedroom in my condo. "Matter of fact—didn't you tell me you was thinking of getting a roommate—maybe even two roomies since you got three bedrooms?"

I didn't need the reminder—the daggers in her eyes were aimed at me.

"Oh, I couldn't," Effie said.

"Sure you can," Becca chimed in. And then, looking at me, said, "Can't she?"

I nodded, wondering if I was biting off too much. I considered Effie's background—as much as I knew—and the accent, pure

Arkansan. The one where they modify the number of actual syllables in a word. Adding ones, like pronouncing name as "neigh-umm." Or using "aye-esk" for ask. Or…the opposite— cutting syllables they deem unnecessary. Fate-vul for Fayetteville.

I don't mind the accent. I've become used to it during my eight years in Arkansas. In some ways it's quite lyrical. The accent wouldn't be a stumbling block to employment, but poor grammar would. Many in my adopted state have difficulty matching plural and singular nouns with the appropriate verbs, tossing in an occasional done went. I tuned my ear to Effie's speech patterns and didn't detect any of those problems. Apparently, she paid attention in school and her words bordered on eloquent. Still, I wondered whether the chore I was assuming would choke me.

On the way out, I told Becca to line up another interview for Effie the next day. Becca's expression told me she thought I was over-extending the equipment.

5

ON THE WAY HOME, EFFIE AND I STOPPED AT THE Second Time Around, a small boutique on the west side of Little Rock near where I live. The owner, Caroline Masters, carries an outstanding selection of one-owner clothing. I've cultivated Caroline for just under two years, and I've found evening gowns as well as business wear there. She likes me and tacks a discount on top of her more-than-reasonable prices.

It took Caroline less than ten minutes to select three outfits, including shoes and handbags, for Effie. She rang up the sale and extended the bill toward Effie. I snatched it from her and said, "This is on me until Effie's paychecks start rolling in." I pulled a pair of twenties from my billfold. "Can you put the rest on my bill—until my checks come in?"

Caroline gave me a knowing smile. She's familiar with my story and knows the tricks my ex pulls. Several months ago I told her Jarvis let me have the condo in the divorce, in the hopes I would default on the mortgage payments. Then he could buy it on the cheap at a foreclosure sale. That's one of the reasons he plays hide-n-seek with the alimony payments.

"Is that son-of-a-bitchen ex husband of yours late again?" Without waiting for a reply, Caroline scribbled "KC" on the bill and tucked it into the register under the cash drawer.

"Caroline, I owe you. Someday, I'll pay you back, big time— for all the times you've carried me."

"You made a big down payment on the favors I've extended right there." She nodded toward Effie, who was admiring herself in a full-length mirror across the room. "I don't know why, but

I know what you're doing. My hunch is, for all your tough talk, you're as big a softie as me."

"Yeah, well—"

"I got into this business the same way you got into working temp jobs." She didn't expand on her side of the story, but said, "I do you a favor, 'cause you're doing a favor for Effie. She'll do a favor for someone else—and eventually, it all will come back to me."

I loved her philosophy. I corralled Effie and a large shopping bag and we headed west on Chenal Parkway, toward my place.

I unlocked the door to my condo and Effie followed me inside. She froze in the doorway staring at the top of the antique hat rack sitting inside the doorway. There's a recessed area at the top and all I could see was a pair of ears and two eyes.

"PK. Behave yourself," I said. PK emitted a low growl, assumed a pose looking like he was ready to pounce and continued staring at us. I snapped my fingers and pointed an index figure at my cat.

Effie said, "Is it dangerous?"

"No, PK likes to see if he can intimidate people. At heart he's a big coward."

"What does PK stand for?"

"Psycho Kitty," I said. The frown on Effie's face told me there was still a question in her mind. "He's a little psychotic. You'll see soon enough, and for all his faults I would be hard put to do without him."

We toured the condo and Effie marveled at the view from the picture window in the living room. The eighth floor is high enough to have a good view toward downtown. She thanked me for taking her in for the night and said, "I don't know where I'll go tomorrow."

"Sometimes I have trouble making the monthly payment on this place. I've been thinking about taking in a roomer who could help me."

She protested she'd never be able to pay me fair market value for the space. Fair market value, I thought. Her vocabulary astounded me. I might have to revise my entire image of Effie. "I wouldn't be asking so much. Besides, I've got two extra bedrooms. I was thinking of taking in a couple of boarders."

We ate a light snack in front of the living room television. A streak of gray launched itself at the far wall.

"What in the world was that?" Effie said.

The wall in question was a mural of a large window looking out over a garden with a small table in the foreground, which appeared to be inside the "room." "PK has never learned the difference between the picture window and the fake one. He thinks he can get up on the table and watch the world go by in the mural. Every so often he races for it, leaps, goes splot against the wall and slides down to the floor like he just did."

"Doesn't he hurt himself?"

"I figure if he does, he'll stop on his own."

We spent the rest of the evening in front of my dressing table. From behind, I watched her in the mirror and coached her on the application of everything from foundation to mascara to lipstick. She was a quick study. I found there was no reason to repeat an instruction. When she finished, I handed her a facial cleanser and asked her to remove all the makeup. When she finished the chore, I said, "Okay. Now put it all back on again."

This time she donned all the cosmetics without coaching. I used the time to drill her on the fine art of an interview. I set a bottle of Reality perfume by Liz Claiborne on the table top. "A small dab of this behind each earlobe will give you the finishing touch in the morning." Though she was pretty enough to use short skirts, I felt she would be more comfortable in the calf-length clothes we purchased.

The next morning, I gave Effie instructions for the bus and enough money for a round trip fare and lunch. I dropped her at a bus shelter and headed for the MAT—the Midtown Atrium Towers. I made it to my new temp job on time—sort of. Mickey's little hand pointed to the "9" and the big hand snapped to the "12" as I pushed through the glass doors.

6

"DO I GET A BRIEFING FROM THE LADY I'M REPLACING?" I said to Cheryl, Cyber-Technology's receptionist. "Mr. Harmon didn't give me much of a run-down yesterday."

"Not unless you want to go to the hospital. She left three days ago—in labor. Sure hope you know accounting, because nobody around here besides Celia does. And like I said, she's in the hospital."

Cheryl led me past a coffee room, a restroom and an office they used for storage. After all that, we arrived at Celia's cubicle. Cheryl pulled a piece of paper from a pocket in her slacks, unfolded it and thrust it toward me. "Wayne told Celia to write down some stuff. I think it tells you the name of her accounting program. Probably shows the password to use to open it and the email files. Beyond that, you're on your own. I been working here four years and I barely know how to turn a computer on."

I figured it would take most of the day learning the computer system and software. Shouldn't be difficult, but with no instructions, much of it would be hit and miss. I did have some background. During the years I spent with Jarvis the Rat, as the "no wife of mine is going to work," I lived the life of the "idle rich." Jarvis made enough money so I could have stayed home eating bon-bons and watching the soaps, which was his fantasy of the ideal wife. Instead, I took every self-improvement course and seminar there was to find. In addition to tai chi, tae kwan do, yoga, karate, firearms and marksmanship training, I wedged in several computer science classes and among instructors I met was a really young guru—and figuring he could be a good resource, I got his internet handle—Crackerjack—and a phone number.

I even took one course about jumping out of airplanes. After the gun courses, I went through the drill of qualifying for a concealed carry permit. The permit's in my purse, but I seldom tote the Glock I purchased back then. I picked a Model 26 for its size. It's a mite shorter than the rest and fits into a purse also purchased at the same time—one with a built-in holster.

I was right about the computer. After stumbling down a few dead ends, by mid-morning I was more than competent with Cyber-Technology's system. I spent my morning break and most of my lunch hour nosing around the Midtown Atrium Towers Building. The "Under Construction" sign in the elevator now displayed yellow crime scene tape pasted over it. Hmmm. Guess they don't want me up there. I'll have to ask Dennis about this development. I ate a small lunch at the snack shop in the lobby. On my way back up to Cyber-Technology, I decided to check the upper floors and the stairwell. In the elevator, I slipped a finger under the sign and pressed the "10" button. When the doors slid open, I found my way blocked by eight to ten strips of crime scene tape across the opening. I wasn't going to break the tape, so I returned to the ninth floor. I pulled the stairwell door on the ninth floor open and stepped through the exit. I checked the other side of the door to be sure I could get back into the ninth floor. I couldn't.

There was a panic bar on the inside, but the stairwell side of the door had a pull handle and no crash bar. No way to open it from the stairs side. You can't get over on a well-trained burglar like me. An old B&E guy I once interviewed for a magazine article taught me to carry a good-size nametag. One with a large metal backing plate, which was held in place by another metal bar with magnets on it. All I needed was the magnetic bar. The idea came from Tony Trees. He carried the moniker from the time he learned not to use his hand to block a door from locking. The door pinched off the pinky on his left hand. At first they called him Three Finger Tony, but with the east coast accent "three" sounded more like "tree." He was Tree Finger Tony until they shortened it, turned it around and he became Tony Trees from then on. He also taught me if I carried the entire nametag, the police would have trouble making a "burglary tools" rap stick. He made sure everything he used for breaking and entering could have a secondary use. By attaching the magnetic bar to the striker plate on the door jamb to cover the hole, the spring lock mechanism has no place to go. The other upside of that type of nametag was it could be worn without punching holes in expensive material.

I removed the magnet from my nametag and slid it onto the striker plate. I tested the arrangement from the inside before I stepped into the stairwell. If the Watergate burglars were as smart as me, there wouldn't have been any masking tape on the lock for a guard to spot.

Satisfied I could escape from the stairwell, I moved up the steps to the tenth floor. The door was locked and crisscrossed with yellow tape. Up to the eleventh floor. Same greeting. I was surprised when I found no tape on the twelfth floor. It didn't even have a stairwell door installed. Ooo-kay. Let's have a look around, Casey.

I moved through sawhorses, scaffolding and stacks of dry-wall and metal wall studs. Even moving with care, my footsteps produced the hollow echo that comes with a large open space. I found my way to what would become the balcony when the floor was built-out. Peering over the railing, I could see the spot on the lobby floor where the body landed—the tape outline was still in place. I leaned farther out, so the planter where the shoe hit was visible. It was a straight vertical drop from the balcony edge to the planter. Why did the shoe go straight down and the body landed around six feet farther out? I didn't have an answer. But then, I didn't have the foggiest notion of the trajectory of bodies and shoes.

I saw a police officer pointing up in my direction. A man who looked like Dennis was hotfooting it toward the elevator.

I beat a hasty retreat to the stairwell and raced back down to the ninth floor. Retrieving my B&E tool from the doorjamb and reassembling my nametag, I hurried around the balcony. I reached the opposite side in time to look up three floors and see Dennis staring over the twelfth-floor railing. He made a wild hand gesture in my direction and I got the impression he wanted me to stay where I was. He was talking on a hand-held radio as he disappeared toward the elevators. Oops. Busted again.

* * *

    I remained on the ninth floor balcony until he arrived. "Dennis. You don't look happy to see me."

"What the hell were you doing up there?"

"Up where?" I knew damn well playing dumb wasn't going to fly, but I loved the exasperated look on his face. I also knew he couldn't prove anything. I'd used a handkerchief on everything I touched. Looking down, I hoped he didn't notice the construction dust on my shoes.

"Don't bullshit me, Casey. What were you doing up there?"

I shrugged my shoulders. "Just looking around. I'm the nosy type. By the way, which floor did old what's-his-name jump off?"

He told me he asked the questions and I was supposed to answer them. That's when I reminded him he no doubt needed all the help he could get. After all, I would be working here with reasonable access to the building grapevine.

He said, "Why should I trust you?"

Winking, I said, "Because I'm cute?"

Dennis grinned and said, "You're more than cute. How about I buy you a cup of coffee?"

I looked at my watch and frowned. "My lunch hour ended ten minutes ago. Make it five-thirty and you can buy me a drink at the bar in the lobby."

"See you then." He turned before I could register surprise, then stopped and faced me. "How the hell did you use the stairwell and get back through the doors?"

I grinned. "For me to know and you to find out." I left him standing in the hallway.

7

ON THE WAY HOME, I MULLED OVER WHAT DENNIS shared with me this afternoon over a Chi-Chi. I learned the dead man was an accountant who worked one floor below Cyber-Tech. His name was Brian Hawkins. I didn't feel so smug when Dennis told me all of it was released to the media the night before. He did share with me the fact they believed Hawkins went over the railing from the tenth floor. He told me he would appreciate it if I'd keep my eyes and ears open. I agreed and asked him if he was going to register me as a Confidential Informant. When he showed surprise, I mentioned the Criminal Justice courses I took last year.

His parting remark was interesting. "If I register you as a CI, I couldn't ask you out on a date."

I hoped my grin didn't make me look senile.

It was close to seven when I got home. Effie was sitting next to my door reading a newspaper.

"Oh, Effie, I'm sorry. I forgot you don't have a key. Come in and we'll fix that right now."

We sat on the couch, and she spent the next twenty minutes regaling me with the details of her new job and how much they were going to pay her.

I interrupted, "Then I guess you got the job."

"Oh…yes. Thanks to you."

That was followed by another twenty minutes describing how the clothes, the makeup and the interview tips helped her. She heaped so much praise on me, I was becoming embarrassed. I did enjoy the warm, inner glow I was feeling. "You're a quick study, Eliza."

"Who?"

I told her the story of Pygmalion and My Fair Lady. She understood the analogy. There was a misty look in her eyes when she reached out and put her arms around my neck.

"I never had a sister," she said. "I've never had anyone like you who cared enough to do anything like this for me."

I decided I spent too many years being a pessimist and misjudging people. Here was a girl I underestimated. At first glance, I figured her for a rough-cut bumpkin who might take years to cultivate. And overnight, my daisy developed into an orchid. Due more to herself, than me.

Effie offered to pay me rent. In my mind, I calculated she was offering over fifty percent of her salary. We settled on a more reasonable figure. She asked if it would be enough, if it would cover my mortgage payment if my alimony was late again.

I was forced to agree the answer to her question was no. I reminded her I was considering a second tenant. After all, there was a separate bath for each of the spare bedrooms. I remember telling Jarvis the Rat, three baths was an extravagance. His response was: let's live it up. One of the few things he did right. Though now I'm sure he would gnash his teeth to learn the extra baths were helping me.

Effie and I put our heads together and came up with a classified ad, "Two women looking for a roomer (prefer thirtyish) to split rent on luxury space in West Little Rock. Large bedroom with private bath. Kitchen privileges. Call for appointment after 6 pm." I added my phone number and headed for the computer. I logged onto the web site for the Democrat Gazette, our major paper in Little Rock. I posted the ad to their online classified section and completed the payment information. "That should bring some responses by tomorrow."

"I can help out with something other than money," Effie said. "I'll do some of the housekeeping chores...and I'm a great cook. You should have a dinner party and let me prepare the meal."

This lady never ceases to amaze me. "A little dusting for now will be fine. Let's hold off on the dinner party." Her doing the cooking would be welcome. Once upon a time I was a fair cook, but of late, meal planning consisted of figuring out how to micro-wave the entree and a veggie at the same time.

I awoke the next morning to the smells of coffee and bacon. Staggering out to the kitchen I saw her. There she was, smiling and happier than a body should be at this hour of the morn-ing. She told me breakfast was the most important meal of the day—her momma always told her that. If she starts warbling like a blue bird, I might have to strangle her. Refusing seconds on everything—eggs, bacon, toast and OJ—I admitted to myself I might get used to breakfast—if I didn't have to fix it. I took another cup of coffee, to be sure my eyes stayed open, and Effie sat down with me.

"How would I look with my hair cut short like yours?" she said.

I took a long look at her hair. It was beautiful, long to the shoulders and a great shade of brown with a hint of auburn. "You might start by having it trimmed a little shorter. Maybe to face length or a bit longer. I chopped mine off all at once and it was a cultural shock for me."

"But you look great."

"I got tired of the habits I developed because I found myself tucking the long hair behind my ears. And, I used a Valley-girl headshake to get it out of my face. One time, I flipped my head so hard I got vertigo. You don't have either of those nasty habits, so take it slow. We can get you an appointment next week if you want."

* * *

This morning, Effie and I took the elevator to the parking garage and climbed into my Mustang. I dropped Effie at her office before heading downtown. Second day on the job I needed to get some real work done. It was time to get a start on the pile of bills stacking up on my desk. My desk? I was already settling in and establishing territorial ownership.

Even though by lunchtime, the stack was negligible, I grabbed a quick snack and returned to the office. It was time to check out the email program. They gave me a password, so I assumed browsing was acceptable. I could have asked Wayne, but I learned a long time ago: if you can't afford a "no" answer, don't ask the question.

My email password gave me access to the accounts of everyone in the office. I created a User Name for myself on Celia's computer and added a password. I knew that approach wouldn't stop any of the guys in this office, but it would give them something to do and would lead them nowhere. I would store any word processing documents or spreadsheets I created under my User Name. If I wanted to hide something, archiving it as a hidden file should do the trick. Again, nothing a dedicated hacker couldn't locate, but these tactics were handy in a previous temp position, so I made a habit of doing it, as a general precaution. Here at Cyber-Tech, all these steps were red herrings. The CD-R drive on Celia's computer offered removable storage, so any personal files I created could be written to a CD-ROM disk or I could use a USB thumb drive. In the past, I found it useful to keep notes about the job and they didn't need to be on the computer itself.

Being the nosy type, like I told Dennis, I browsed through the email folders for the other employees. Every folder contained personal notes, the subject line tended to indicate the general contents, and I checked a couple—to prove to myself I could. Along with those emails, there were a number of inter-office instructions passed along to all the employees.

After reviewing several, I noticed many email subject lines contained a client name with the phrase "C-T Access" tacked on. I opened some of these files but they contained gibberish; marketing information, I thought and made a mental note to bring a thumb drive from home the next day. The one I was thinking of contained a decryption program.

* * *

Even though I left work at six, I found Effie beat me home. "No one waited until six o'clock to call. I returned a couple," she said. "Two people are coming over tonight. They're looking for a place to stay."

That's pretty cheeky, I thought. Checking my answering machine, returning calls and making appointments. "Did I have any personal calls?" She shook her head and I figured, what the hey. Effie's an intelligent lady and I better get used to having someone underfoot—full time.

As Effie and I watched the late-night news, we discussed the two candidates we interviewed this evening. Neither seemed to be a fit and I was polite but firm as I declined their offers to share rent.

"I don't think PK liked them either," Effie said. "Did you see the way he sat on the end table and stared at them?"

We enjoyed a good laugh and I said, "I didn't think it would be this hard to find a roomer. Maybe I was being too picky. Hope tomorrow's a better day."

8

I WAS ON TIME AGAIN WHEN I ARRIVED AT WORK
the following morning. I do pride myself for being punctual…
most of the time. Once I learned the routine, my workload at
Cyber-Technology was light. By nine forty-five, I was caught up
on accounts payable and accounts receivable. I took a small stack
of checks to Wayne for his signature. He wasn't in his office, so
I left them in the middle of the desktop.

I headed downstairs to enjoy a latte at the coffee bar in the
lobby. I was sipping my drink and scanning the morning paper
when I heard the scream. I looked up in time to see a woman,
the shriek still coming from her mouth, pointing up. This time,
I saw the body before it hit the lobby floor. Even from about fifty
feet away, something about the man looked familiar. I recognized the rather garish electric-blue sport coat Ross Worthington
was wearing this morning. "My God!" I jumped up and started
toward the body. A security guard beat me to it, and held his
arms out in a "don't pass" posture. I stood stock-still and gaped.
"My God. It's a man from the office I work in…"

The guard reached for his walkie-talkie. "What's his name?
Where do you work?" He repeated my answers into his radio
and motioned other bystanders to stay clear.

* * *

After my first day in this building, I didn't think I would ever
be sad to see Dennis Epstein. He must have recognized my dis-
tress. After he asked why I'd been in the lobby, he took my arm as

I led him back to the table where I was sitting when Ross fell to his death. My latte was still there, but it held no interest for me.

Today I got the full run-down from Dennis. He pumped me for everything I knew about Worthington, which was precious little. Then he filled me in on the first man to die. His name was Brian Hawkins—which I already knew—and he worked for Boneventure, Smith & Carsten, LLC, an accounting firm on the eighth floor. "The one we can rule out from the Boneventure firm is Wesley Smith. He died about five years ago."

His attempt at humor was welcome, if not effective. "You sure Hawkins took a header from the tenth floor? That's one floor above where I work."

"We found a few footprints and signs of a scuffle in the dust. It did seem like someone swept the floors—maybe trying to cover evidence of them being there. Both floors above seemed pretty clean. The construction people haven't done any work there for at least two weeks. No tenants waiting for space."

"Does it seem strange the floors involved in this are one flight above and below where I work?"

"Are you confessing, Casey?"

"No…I just…I mean it seems strange, that's all." Then I saw the smile on his face. "Okay. For that you have to buy me dinner."

"I'd love to. Can't make it tonight. How about tomorrow?"

I pretended to check my calendar and said yes.

"I'll pick you up about seven-thirty."

* * *

Before I got home, Effie was busy again. She screened one prospective roomer over the phone. "Sounded too aggressive to me," she said. "The other one may be a good fit. She was calling on a cell phone, and I couldn't hear her very well. Her name is Dante Kincaid. She'll be here at eight."

Boy, life was getting easy. The dinner Effie was preparing on the stove smelled delicious, and here she was playing secretary—guarding my privacy and setting appointments. I could get used to a life of leisure.

"Isn't Dante kind of a funny name for a woman?" Effie said.

"I suppose so. No worse than Acacia."

"Who's Acacia?"

It dawned on me Effie didn't know my real first name. Over dinner I went through my name change and the evolution from Acacia to KC to Casey.

The doorbell rang at five till eight. "At least she's punctual," Effie said and headed toward the door. She pulled it open. "Oh…"

I looked up at the object of her "Oh" and saw a tall, slim but well built, good looking black man.

"Okay if I come in?" he said.

I jumped forward trying to cover our lack of civility. I knew it was already too late. "I'm sorry…Mr.…Mr.…"

"Kincaid," he said.

"Yes I know, but I was expecting a…a female. Ah…come in and sit down." I took a chair opposite the couch. He looked far more comfortable than I would have expected.

He looked around the condo and walked to the window before he headed for the couch. "You have a fantastic view. I'd love to live here."

Effie stood near the door taking in the entire scene, but not moving. "Come on over and sit down, Effie," I said. She took the second chair facing the couch. PK came wandering in from my bedroom and made his usual living room entrance—streak of gray, leap, splot, slide down the wall.

Kincaid didn't bat an eye. He said, "What a fine example of a trompe l'oeil. No wonder the cat is fooled by it."

I sat there without the slightest notion of what a "trump loyal" was. Any minute now Effie will ask him, maybe. Just when I need her, she's a stone statue. I couldn't stand not knowing and said, "It's quite a what?"

He apologized and said. "A trompe l'oeil is a style of decorating using realistic looking paintings. In French, a literal translation is 'deceive the eye.' "

I did something with my shoulders and head, which was meant to convey—of course, I knew that. It seemed to fail and I waved him toward the couch.

When Kincaid took a seat, I said, "Again, Mr. Kincaid, I…we were expecting a woman. Our ad said two ladies were looking for a roommate."

PK shook off the encounter with the wall and made his way to the couch where Kincaid sat. I started to warn him PK might bat at his hand if he tried to pet the cat. I was too late. PK was rubbing against his legs and then stood still for a neck rub.

"Exactly so," he said. "I didn't see anything in the advertisement restricting the applicants to the female gender."

He made his statement and shut up. He dumped it back on me and I'm sure he knew it. And, I'm sure he was waiting to see what sort of story I would come up with. His hand dangled over the arm of the sofa and PK was skulking toward it. I was about to warn the poor man again when PK arched his back and rubbed Mr. Kincaid's hand. He looked down and petted PK on the head and then stroked the cat's chin and throat. PK was purring loud enough for everyone to hear. I was taken by surprise—"PK usually doesn't take to strangers."

I invented a couple of arguments based on the condominium association's rules. He countered each as if there was a copy of the by laws in his pocket. With no reason left, I said, "It boils down to the boy-girl issue."

"I don't see that as a problem," Dante said. "I can assure you I am looking for shelter, not co-habitation. Even if I was, you'd have nothing to fear from me."

What? I'm not his type? Despite everything, I liked this man. He was straightforward and honest. I was assuming the honesty part. He was quiet for a moment, then he said, "You're the lady who saw the men fall to their deaths at the MAT building, aren't you?"

It was more of a statement than a question. "How did you know?" I said.

"I've got a lot of friends—all over town—who owe me favors."

"Wait a minute," Effie said looking at our visitor. "You used 'saw the men fall' a plural reference. I didn't know there was a second one, Casey."

I looked at Effie and said, "Oh, good grief. I've been so disconcerted all day I forgot to tell you about the guy from my office. He took a dive like the first one."

Not wanting to get into a long discussion in front of Kincaid, I held up a hand to Effie and said, "Later." To our visitor I said, "Dante, leave your references and let me talk it over with Effie. I'll let you know in the morning."

He left and I remembered I didn't check the mail on my way up this evening. Effie accompanied me and we found Kenley in the lobby. He held the elevator as I emptied the mailbox and hurried back.

He pressed the button for our floor and said, "How did you like Dante?" The look on my face must have registered surprise because he added, "I met him in the lobby and rode up with him earlier. He's quite a fine young man. We learned a lot about one another in a short elevator ride."

"He was nice," Effie said, "but we're sort of worried about the boy-girl arrangement."

Kenley smiled like he knew something we didn't. "I think you'll have no fear on that score. He's gay."

"Oh, yes," Effie said. "He was quite humorous."

"No, my dear. Not funny…gay. As in lifestyle." Kenley smiled his smile again.

I watched Effie as the gears in her head slipped, spun, then caught and took hold.

She said, "Oh…"

Back inside the condo, we talked about our prospective room-mate and I asked Effie why she didn't ask Dante what a "trump loyal" was.

"I already knew," she said. "I figured you did too."

The late news came on and I watched the program through the weathercast for the following day. "That's it for me," I said. "Let's sleep on Dante and make a decision in the morning." I realized what I'd said and saw Effie grinning at me. We enjoyed a good laugh and started toward our bedrooms.

9

EVEN THOUGH IT WAS SATURDAY, WAYNE HARMON asked everyone to come in to work. Some B.S. about overdue client reports. I told him I would be happy to work as well.

Now it was morning, and I was sorry about postponing the decision. It still faced me. And, I wasn't sure it was a good idea to bring in a black, gay male as a roomer.

"Don't be an old fuddy-duddy," Effie said over breakfast. "I think Dante's a fine person. And, besides I've never known a gay person before. I could probably learn something from him."

Never knew a gay before? I thought. Bet you've known some, and they never admitted the fact. She was wearing me down. "Okay," I said. "But I'll have to check his references first." I wondered about her comment of learning from him. Maybe she wanted to broaden her horizons. Maybe she's smarter than I, and I should say yes to Dante.

* * *

The office was still in an uproar this morning. With Ross Worthington's death the previous day, the employees in both buildings and the ones working weekends, were abuzz with rumors like: Worthington's death was a copycat killing. The police were again swarming over all the floors.

"I pretended I needed to talk to you," Dennis Epstein said. "Unless you've remembered something about either death, I wanted to check to be sure we were still on for tonight."

I nodded. "Dennis, what would you think if I told you Effie and I were thinking of taking in another roomer? A black, gay man."

I looked at Dennis. His raised eyebrows and a head tilted down as if looking over a pair of specticals told me he wasn't sure what I was talking about. With a slight headshake he said, "What's his name?"

When I told him it was Dante Kincaid, he said, "You mean Aaron?"

"No. Dante."

"His first name is Aaron. Dante is his middle name."

Now I was confused. Dennis laughed and told me Aaron was a friend of his partner.

"Ah, ha! So that's how he knew about me working here. Back to my original question. How would he be as a roommate?"

"I don't think you could make a better choice."

After the ringing endorsement from Dennis, the reference calls about Dante—Aaron—seemed superfluous. I made them anyway. Aaron Dante Kincaid was indeed employed by an airline as a flight attendant. He listed four years in the Air Force under military service. He was an outstanding employee. His personal references all agreed his character was beyond reproach. Oh, well. That's what references are supposed to tell you.

A glance at the clock told me I'd wasted about thirty minutes. I think I made up my mind before the calls. Two more calls to make.

I told Effie our new roomie, Aaron—Dante—would be moving in. When I called Aaron, he was surprised to hear me call him by his first name, but was pleased with my decision. I told him he could move in tonight if he liked.

* * *

Dennis picked me up at seven-thirty and drove us to the Peabody Hotel in downtown Little Rock. The maitre d' seated us and Dennis ordered for both of us. I'm not used to so much controlling since Jarvis walked out, and I'm not sure I want to get used to it.

The conversation drifted to the MAT building and the two men who died. "Casey, I think you must be confused about when you heard the shoe drop." I shook my head and he said, "You sure? Because, it's the only detail stopping us from stamping Case Closed on the first death."

"Then how the hell did the shoe come off?"

Dennis thought for a moment, then said, "Probably shouldn't be giving out details like this, but he was wearing loafers. No laces to untie and we figure he banged his foot on the railing as he went over and the shoe came off."

"That still doesn't explain why it landed several seconds after the body hit. If it came off like you say it did, it should have landed at the same time as the body…shouldn't it?"

Dennis looked like he wanted to agree, but he didn't say anything. Then he added, "I think you must be confused about the shoe landing after the body hit."

I shook my head. "Seems to me the best explanation for the shoe's late arrival is someone dropping it…after the body went over."

The expression on his face told me he wished he wasn't involved in this discussion. "We didn't get any forensic evidence, which points to a second person."

"So maybe there is some evidence, but it's not conclusive?"

"I can't say any more," Dennis said.

I decided to press the point. "If he killed himself, then how the hell do you explain the second murder? What possible motives do you have for two men to leap over a tenth floor railing?"

He opened his mouth, but I held up my hand. "Two men in a couple of days jump to their deaths. Seems to be a convenient coincidence. Do you believe in coincidences?" Before he could respond, I kept at it. "I only knew Worthington for a short while, but he didn't seem depressed. Did either have financial problems?"

Dennis shook his head. I said, "Then what the hell are you basing your decisions on?…WAGs?" Dennis looked puzzled. "Wild Ass Guesses," I said.

I must have sounded ticked off—which I was. Dennis didn't say anything and continued eating.

"Well?" I said.

"I don't know what to say, Casey. No, I don't usually believe in coincidences, but sometimes, shit happens. And, who the hell are you to question me about my case? Who died and appointed you boss?"

I wished I hadn't gone quite so far, but that water was well past the bridge. I figured the evening was about over. We finished dessert, left the restaurant and Dennis dropped me in front of my condo building. If I'd counted the words we spoke on the way home, I wouldn't have needed a second hand.

10

BY THE TIME I GOT UP THE ELEVATOR AND INTO MY residence, there was a message waiting for me on the answering machine. "Casey, this is Dennis. I'm sorry the evening ended on such a sour note. I hope this wasn't the end of…of whatever it is. We probably shouldn't talk anymore tonight—I'll give you a call tomorrow."

On my way to my bedroom, I could see signs of Aaron's move-in while I was at dinner.

* * *

Sunday morning didn't do anything to improve my disposition. I opened my drapes and watched the sun lighten the horizon behind a thick blanket of clouds. It was going to be a dark gloomy day filled with rain. PK, sensing my mood, headed for one of his favorite hiding places—on the top shelf of my closet, way up out of sight.

Effie did her best to lighten the mood. Nobody in their right mind is that perky at this hour on a rainy day. Aaron was somewhere between these extreme moods. I figured it was due to his job as a flight attendant—having to put up with all manner of creeps aboard his plane.

I complained to everyone who would listen. Since I am the landlord, it meant Effie and Aaron would have to sit through my tirade.

Over breakfast, I told them about my evening with Dennis. They agreed it seemed like the police were trying to wrap up the deaths using the easiest way out.

I was still mad at Dennis. I shouldn't have questioned his deductive abilities, but I was upset my eyewitness statement was being dismissed.

By late morning, the anger began to dissipate and there was time to take a breath or two between sentences. There were looks of hope on both their faces.

I leaned back, took a sip of coffee and said, "Well, if the police don't want to look into a pair of murders, I'll solve the damn case myself."

I was surprised at the reaction I saw. Their faces mirrored one another. At first there was disbelief—eyes darting side to side. Then, a self-satisfied look and a smile. Aaron said, "Let's go get 'em, Casey." And Effie added, "Count me in."

I said, "Alexander Dumas, move over—"

"The Three Musketeers ride again," Effie said.

That girl's a surprise a minute, I thought.

Aaron glanced at his watch. "It's almost noon. What say I throw some lunch together?"

"Be there in a minute," I said. "I've got to toss some clothes in the washer." When I got to the kitchen, I had the feeling those two were hatching something.

Opening my mouth, Aaron beat me to it and said, "I'm leaving tomorrow morning. Be gone for three days, but when I get back on Wednesday, I'll check with the police. Casey, you seem determined to snoop until you get into trouble. I might as well keep you company."

Effie chimed in, "I want to help, too. This could be like a Nancy Drew mystery. What should we name our whodunit?"

Over lunch, it took fifteen minutes, but we decided to call it: The Case of the Plunging Bodies. With three of us working together, we cleaned up the dishes in record time and settled in the living room. I went over every detail I could remember, from the time I entered the Midtown Atrium Towers Building the first day, up to the time Dennis dropped me off last night. "Damn. I didn't even get a chance to see the ducks promenade from the lobby to the elevator. We got there too late for the parade."

Aaron laughed. "I didn't know you had a thing for ducks, Casey. Earlier you said, 'find the killer.' Why singular? Two dead guys. Couldn't there be two killers?"

"I suppose if the killings are unrelated, we are looking for two. The police think the second was a copycat, albeit a suicide. If it was murder, it could be a copycat."

Aaron said, "Then we need to find a motive for the first death."

Effie leaned forward. "What if the first killing was the copycat? I mean, what if it was done first to cover up the real motive—the reason to kill Mr. Worthington?"

"Well, we've really narrowed that down," I said. "We have one or two motives. If there are two motives, we have to find two murderers. If there is a single motive and killing—meaning only one killer—which killing was real and which one was the cover up?"

The phone rang and I punched a button on the cordless. It was Dennis, so I retreated to my bedroom and closed the door. When I returned to the living room, two expectant faces stared at me.

"Okay," Aaron said. "Give. Is all forgiven? Is there still hope for Dennis after all?"

I nodded and told them we'd agreed to disagree, and I got a rain check for another dinner next week. Since I was planning on some snooping tomorrow, I put a few extra items in my purse.

11

THIS IS MY FIFTH DAY ON THE JOB AT Cyber-Technology, and I've got the work routine down pat. I breezed through the accounts receivable pile and printed the necessary dun letters, put them in my out-basket and attacked accounts payable. Company policy was never miss a discount deadline, but don't pay anything sooner than need be. I stacked the checks needing Wayne's signature on the corner of my desk and reached for my purse.

I pulled out the thumb drive I stored in my purse at home last Friday, the day Worthington died. That day was so hectic, I didn't get around to the job. I slipped the thumb drive into the USB port on the computer tower under my desk. I accessed a program on that drive and pointed it toward the folders where the company emails resided. The program attacked the gibberish in the emails and ground through the algorithms that would decode the contents of the encrypted messages. Once the first message was translated, the next took but a few seconds. It looked like C-T was using a single encryption routine without any variations and it seemed to be a simple key. My super-sleuth program was decoding emails faster than I could copy the results onto my computer.

As I worked, I noticed the messages were short. Many of them just two words. I knew the folder I created as a hidden one would not fool any expert for long. I planned to transfer its contents back to the thumb drive. It would be dangerous to leave the files on this computer. I didn't expect to find anything of interest in the C-T emails, but most employers don't like temps messing around sensitive company business. I could examine them at home.

My final step was using another program written by a friend of mine to wipe the empty spaces on my computer's hard drive. The program was designed to write and erase several times over the blank spots on the drive foiling any attempt to recover the deleted material. My friend assured me it exceeded the Department of Defense requirements for erasing classified information.

I was about to "wipe" the hard drive when Wayne burst around the corner of my cubicle. I hit the Windows key and the "M" key at the same time and before my monitor was visible to him, the programs were minimized and the desktop didn't show what was running. My taskbar was set to "auto-hide" mode so it wasn't visible to indicate what was active.

Wayne said, "I thought I'd save you a trip to my office and pick up the outgoing checks."

"They're right there," I said pointing to the stack on the corner of my desk. "I was just about to start on the accounts receivable letters," I lied.

He grabbed the checks and headed back to his office. I gave him fifteen minutes, which was enough time to have completed the dun letters. It was also more than adequate for running the "wipe" program and stashing the USB thumb drive in my purse.

I put the letters on Wayne's desk and told him I was taking an early lunch. Rather than going downstairs, I headed for the ninth floor staircase. With my nametag back in place on the door jamb, I started up the stairs for the tenth floor. There, the crime scene tape was still in place and the door was locked. Same thing on the eleventh floor. At twelve, the door was still missing but yellow tape was added. I popped the end of one piece of tape loose and eased through the opening. Not much changed, I thought. Same old stacks of build-out materials.

I did notice sets of footprints in the construction dust. It seemed like more prints than last time. I moved to the balcony area on the side opposite from where the men fell to their deaths. I crouched down and eased forward. I wanted to see the railing area on the tenth floor without being visible to anyone below.

I pulled a small pair of binoculars from my purse. Perhaps purse is a misnomer. A boyfriend once referred to this particular one as a saddlebag. It wouldn't fit over a horse's rump, but it could never be confused with an evening clutch.

Even the three-power magnification the little binoculars provided did little for the view. Damn, I wish I could nose around the tenth floor. A crash sounded off to my right like a metal wall stud hitting the concrete floor. My pulse picked up a good thirty beats per minute, and I sidled fast to my left toward the stairwell I used for entry. I didn't see anyone there or on my way back to the ninth floor. I reassembled my nametag and entered the Cyber-Technology office. I waited a couple more minutes to get my breathing under control before heading down to the lobby.

"Where the hell have you been?" It was Eberheart and his face seemed flushed.

"Just been out for a potty break." Lame, but better than nothing.

He glowered at me and said, "Order me a new Cyber-Technology ID badge. I think mine was stolen at a client's office."

I almost asked him where the badges came from and thought better of it. His mood didn't indicate helpfulness. There must be something in the files about it, so all I said was, "Yes, sir. I'll get right on it."

Eberheart stalked out of my cubicle and was out of sight in seconds.

I took the elevator to the lobby. As I crossed the marble tile toward the cafe a familiar voice said, "Casey?" I looked around to see my benefactor from my first day here, Gene Morse, smiling at me.

"I was here on business," he said. "You still working here?"

I said yes and he shuffled around and at last asked if we could have dinner sometime. The "I'm involved" line is ineffectual, but it worked and I excused myself from any dinner plans. "If you have the time, I suppose we could have lunch here," I said and pointed to the cafe. He nodded.

As we ate, I learned he was an accountant and was here to see a client. I said I didn't think CPAs made house calls. He muttered saying sometimes he needed to get out and beat the bushes for clients. I smiled, hoping it would be taken for nothing more than one from a friend and inquired where his office was located. He started with some vague directions and then veered off the subject. I spent most of the lunch hour answering his questions about me and he got far more information on me than I learned about him.

We parted in the lobby and I saw him glance over his shoulder at me as he neared the doors to the street. There was an uneasy feeling in my stomach. For a moment, I wondered if Gene was somehow involved in the murders. Hell, Casey, I thought. For sure he can't be the one who pushed Brian Hawkins over the rail. Gene was in the lobby with me. Of course, I don't know where he was when Ross Worthington took his header three days later. I shrugged, doing my best impression of shaking something off my back.

12

YESTERDAY AND TODAY WERE UNEVENTFUL. I STAYED put in the Cyber-Technology office and didn't venture to the upper floors. I used my computer to nose around C-T's main server, but learned little I didn't already know. When I got back home, Aaron was already there. He'd returned from his overnight turn-around flights and stopped at the Little Rock Police Department on his way home. He told me he talked with Dennis' partner. "He and I are old friends," he said.

I raised an eyebrow in a question.

He took a while to respond. "Oh…no. He's just a friend. We played on the same ball team back in the day…does it make a difference?"

He caught me off guard. "No," I said, "It's just…It's…no. No difference." I figured the exchange sent the wrong message. Oh, hell. I'm not sure what message I do want to send.

The smell of coffee brewing sent us scurrying to the kitchen. Effie placed food on the kitchen table and poured the aromatic brew into mugs. She insisted it was nothing but leftovers. Her toss-togethers looked like something I would spend a major portion of the day preparing.

Over dinner, Aaron covered his visit to the LRPD. The police had not advanced any new theories. They were stuck on the suicide idea for both deaths.

PK made the rounds under the table, rubbing against legs and making one of his more pleasant sounds. Having checked out all of us, he chose Aaron and hopped up onto his lap. He sat there allowing Aaron to rub his neck and the top of his head.

"They have to be the most stupid oafs I've ever met," I said. "Are they capable of finding their own butts if they get to use both hands?"

Effie leaned forward. "That may not be fair, Casey. I bet they didn't tell Aaron everything they know."

I cocked my head toward her. "One of these days that trusting attitude will get you in big trouble."

Effie leaned back and looked like she'd shrunk two dress sizes. I mentally kicked myself in the rear and thought, in a matter of a few minutes I've insulted and belittled both of these two.

Aaron continued describing his visit to the police station. As he wound down, he said, "They didn't say this outright. But, I got the impression they'd like you to keep nosing around the MAT building, Casey."

"What do they think I can do—be the moving target in the arcade?"

Aaron shook his head. "These are vibes, not facts. I got the feeling they think if they investigate openly, they'll drive any perps underground."

"Perps?" Effie said.

"Yeah, perpetrators," Aaron said. "Hang around a bunch of cops and you start sounding like them. My hunch is they figure you might be able to pick up something on the secretary's grapevine."

"I've suspected the same, but the way you put it is pretty damn sexist. That your term or theirs?"

Aaron did a palms-toward-me number. "Don't shoot. Just repeating the facts ma'am."

That broke me up. "Okay, Sergeant Friday, you're off the hook—you do remember 'Dragnet' don't you?" We all laughed and the relationship cordiality rose to room temperature or better. "I still wonder about their motives—the police in general and Dennis in particular."

"I'm wondering if Cyber-Technology's clients are having continuing problems," I said. "I'm not sure if C-T is doing follow-ups with the same clients or not. It seems like I see a lot of accounts receivable payments from the same customers."

Effie jumped up. "What do you want to know about them?"

I rattled off a list: What sort of computer problems are they having? Same ones recurring or are they different? Are their problems company-wide or isolated to a few computers, or a single computer? I looked at Effie. She wasn't taking any notes, so I figured her initial question was rhetorical. Even so, I kicked out a couple more questions.

After a long pause, Effie said, "Is there anything else?" I shook my head and she added, "I'll need the names of the companies."

I pulled out the list I jotted down at work and handed it to her. Her eyes scanned down the names of about thirty companies. She nodded to herself and said, "I ought to be able to get the answers from at least half of them tomorrow."

I rolled my eyes and said a mental, Yeah! Right.

I wasn't sure if there was a note of skepticism in Aaron's voice when he said, "How are you going to get anything from those companies? You don't know them …"

"I don't think it'll be a problem. I can sound like a real friend on the phone. I'm even better in person, but with this much to research, I'll have to call them." Her index and middle fingers danced through the air. "You know. Let your fingers do the walking."

I did another eye roll.

Effie looked at the two of us. "Would you mind doing the dishes? Looks like I've got some homework."

I didn't include the addresses on the client list, so Effie settled in at the dining room table with the phone directory. Then, she disappeared into the den and I could hear the computer keyboard clickity-clacking.

When Aaron and I emerged from the kitchen, he kicked the recliner back and reached for the TV remote. Surfing channels, he looked for a sports show and settled on an NBA game. I sank into my favorite chair, the one facing the large picture widow. I could see the lights of downtown and from the MAT building. I've thought about that place enough for tonight, I said to myself. I reached for the mystery I was reading.

At ten p.m., I asked Aaron to switch to local news. I responded to his pained expression with, "I've been keeping one eye on the game—the score isn't even close." I watched the tube through the weather so I could figure out what to wear in the morning. On the way to bed, I peeked in on Effie. She was absorbed on the internet, scribbling notes and printing web pages. She didn't hear my "good night."

13

THE NEXT MORNING, THE THREE OF US SAT AROUND the kitchen table discussing our plans for the day. Aaron didn't have to work and said he'd head downtown to police headquarters again. Effie would have two break periods and her lunch hour to contact the people on the client list I gave her. I didn't hold much hope she would gather any useful information.

After my shower, I put on black slacks and a light gray blouse. Slacks would be better for prowling around the upper floors of the MAT building. I was standing in front of the vanity applying makeup when my choice of clothes hit me. Rummaging around the construction debris would stir up dust and black pants would show every speck.

I broke off in the middle of applying lipstick and headed for my closet. I selected a beige blouse with pearl buttons and medium tan slacks, then went back to the bathroom to finish the lip work. A pair of brown, medium-heel boots and a navy blazer finished off the ensemble and I headed for the living room. Effie was waiting and we left for work.

Kenley Longstreet, from my floor, joined us for the ride down to the lobby. "I haven't seen much of young Aaron since he moved in," he said.

"Do I detect a note of interest in your voice?" I said.

Kenley was looking toward me, but his eyes were focused way out there where the buses don't run. He said, "Ah, it would be a pleasant relationship, but, alas, I greatly fear he is presently engaged."

I was surprised, because Aaron gave no indication there was a significant other. Kenley got off the elevator at the lobby, and

Effie and I rode down to the parking garage. I dropped Effie at her work and drove on into downtown. I checked over my right shoulder and saw a darkening sky indicating a row of storms tracking up I-30 from Texarkana heading into town. The rain was moving into the area like the weatherman predicted last night. I smiled to myself. I wouldn't need the umbrella I kept on the back seat because underground garages have their benefits. Today was going to be a scorcher, not so much for the temperature, but for the humidity. Late July in Little Rock can be oppressive with weather you can wear.

The construction on the interstate didn't seem to slow the storm front. The first fat splots hit my hood and windshield and did battle with the dust and pollen accumulated on the car. A heavy shower hit as I whipped into the underground parking area at the MAT building. I used a key-card and swung into the parking place reserved for Ross Worthington. I knew the number assigned to the slot because I discovered it in his personnel records in the C-T office. That's also where I discovered the key-card Ross carried when he was alive. I assumed the police returned his personal effects to C-T since there were no known relatives. I figured since Ross took a header from the tenth floor, he wouldn't need the parking space. Besides, it's great to be able to leave the car in a shady location in Little Rock in the summer. I also figured I'd better mention this arrangement to my temp boss, Wayne Harmon. I was sure he would be okay with it, but it's always better not to surprise the boss.

The stack of checks coming in and going out was larger than usual. Most of the morning slipped away before I glanced up at the clock. It was ten-thirty and I almost missed Cheryl's morning coffee break. I wanted to pump her for anything she knew about the company and the principals. I closed the computer program I was working on and hurried toward the front.

Cheryl grabbed a cordless phone and was heading for the glass doors to the office. I joined her and asked if she minded company for her morning coffee break. We could have used the small break room in the C-T offices, but agreed a latte from Starbucks in the lobby was preferable to C-T's watered-down coffee. I looked down at the phone she was holding and said, "Does that thing let you handle calls while you're out of the office?"

"It works okay in the break room and restroom, but it's not so hot clear down in the lobby…the answering service kicks in after the fourth ring anyway, so I don't miss much."

"Cheryl, how did you land this job with Cyber-Technology?" By the time we reached the ground floor, she covered her earliest days through high school and at least three boyfriends. Her first two jobs out of school were ancient history by the time we reached the coffee shop. With the two drinks between us at a small table, Cheryl went through three more boyfriends and a couple more jobs before we reached modern history. "…then I came here for an interview. Wayne…Mr. Harmon said I possessed all the attributes I needed and he hired me on the spot."

Looking at Cheryl, I agreed she did have all the attributes. Besides being able to remember the company name and say hello, she bulged and curved in all the right places. She seemed proud of her endowments—she seldom hid much of her boobs. Most of her clothing was low cut and skirts stopped short of her knees. What the hell? I told myself. I use the same short hemline on occasion to my own advantage. She wasn't the brightest bulb in the knife drawer, but she wasn't stupid either. She paid attention to what happened in the office and didn't seem shy about sharing the information. I eased her into a conversation about the main players at C-T.

Cheryl sipped her drink and shared everything she knew about her bosses. I didn't learn much except—they all seemed to have a lot more money after the Millennium Bug scare. Business picked up and clients were running out their ears. She didn't complain since they shared their good fortune with her in the form of raises and bonuses. They hired several more employees—at least she thought they were employees. They were on the payroll even though she seldom saw them. Once in a while, new faces would appear at the front desk, disappear into the boss's office, and then leave as fast as they came. I also learned she didn't think Wayne Harmon was the boss even though he occupied the front office,.

I probed for details, and Cheryl seemed to get nervous. I was afraid I was scaring her off, so I jumped to another subject. "So, how's your love life. Mine's in the toilet." That brought a smile to her face and the chitchat continued. We talked for another twenty minutes and I kept the conversation focused away from Cyber-Technology. Her relationships with the opposite sex were not nearly as lackluster as mine.

She stopped talking and asked me about my history. I told her about supporting Jarvis through law school, about the stay-at-home life Jarvis decreed for me and how I hated it. I described the new secretary who worked for him—the one he chased around the desk until she let him catch her.

"What was her name?" she asked.

"Honest to God, you won't believe this. I don't know whether her parents were Walt Disney fans or whether they wanted a four-legged forest critter instead of a kid, but they named her... Bambi."

"No way."

"Way."

"He sounds like a total butthead," Cheryl said.

"You won't get an argument from me on that account."

By the time we headed back upstairs, she knew most of the details of my so-called life with Jarvis the Rat. We commiserated all the way up on the elevator.

"How come the judge was so pissed off at him?" Cheryl said.

We stopped in the hallway, and I described the day in court when my ex screwed himself to the table in front of the judge. "His ego got in the way and he represented himself in our divorce hearing. First, he brought Bambi into the courtroom and she sat at his table. Our judge was a female, and she didn't seem enamored when she asked Jarvis to introduce his co-counsel. He said she wasn't an attorney, but he was training her to be a paralegal. He told the judge her name. The judge did a double-take, an eye roll and shrugged her shoulders. He was off to a bad start and it got worse when he referred to me as the bitch."

Cheryl did a shimmy-squirm and a big smile was spreading across her face.

"I was watching the judge when he uttered those words, and she shot lighting and thunderbolts at him with her eyes, but Jarvis wasn't paying attention—he was on a roll and enthralled with his own voice. The second time he referred to 'Casey the bitch,' I knew he was in trouble up to his Grecian Formula'd widow's peak. The judge let him have it with both barrels. He objected, the judge overruled. He tried to present his evidence and the judge ruled it inadmissible. Decisions were all going my way."

I took a moment to let this last bit soak in. Cheryl's lips pursed and her eyes widened. I think she was picturing herself enjoying the tale as if watching in the courtroom.

"The judge mentioned a maintenance figure and he objected. The judge doubled the figure and asked him he'd like to go double or nothing again. I could have sworn she looked at me and winked, but I'm sure it was my imagination. All my attorney needed to do was sit back and let Jarvis step into the abyss he created. He did an admirable job of hanging himself and verbal disembowelment comes to mind. Healthy monthly stipend, healthy lump-sum settlement and he volunteered the condo. I found out later he was hoping I would default on the mortgage and he could pick it up for a few bucks. That's why he's late with the alimony checks most months."

Cheryl was pressing forward even further, I was concerned her ample attributes were going to impale me—I took a step backward. She looked like she was hoping for more.

"I have to meet someone for lunch, but let's get together again for our afternoon break," I said.

She nodded and went into the C-T offices. I was fibbing about lunch. I planned an excursion up to the top floors, so I could look for a way into the tenth floor. I couldn't imagine what the police might have missed, but I wanted to satisfy my own curiosity.

By eleven-thirty, with my desk clear, I checked out of the office on my lunch break. I headed for the stairwell door. I employed the nametag trick and scooted up the stairs. The police tape at the doors on ten and eleven was still in place and the doors were locked. On twelve, I went through the doorless entry, being careful not to disturb the yellow strips of tape. Fifteen minutes later, I'd covered all the ground again, but this time I paused at a pile of something covered with a tarp. It was against an outside wall and a long way from the active construction. When I pulled the covering up, I discovered it was not material but a framework to keep workers from falling down the hole in the floor. I peered into the darkness and decided this hole and the one below it led to the tenth floor. I looked at the ladder leading down. Ladder was an exaggerated description for that piece of equipment. It consisted of a pair of two-by-sixes with one-by-fours nailed to them forming rungs. Cobbled was a more apt term for how it was thrown together.

I eased my way down to the floor below and made a quick tour of the level. Ten minutes told me all I needed to know. More debris from the suspended build-out much like the floor above. The next ladder led me down to the tenth floor. That was where I hoped to find something. What did I expect to find? The question turned over and over in my mind as I made my way around. I ended at the point by the railing where both bodies were assumed to have made their final leap. Except—I still believed they were "helped" over the railing.

I got down on my hands and knees examining the floor. Next, I turned my attention to the railing, which was wood-topped metal with vertical bars welded to a horizontal support beam a couple of inches off the concrete. Except for the wood topper, the metal was still raw, rough with exposed weld joints, all waiting for a final burnishing and the finish coat of paint.

I began examining the railing in detail, covering it from the top down. Along the wood, there seemed to be scuffmarks toward the center of the span where the bodies slid over the top. I checked all the vertical bars and switched my inspection to the bottom support working toward the middle, when I saw something brown against the bare metal. As I knelt forward for a better look, I heard something or someone moving around.

I didn't wait to identify the noises and beat another hasty retreat back to the ladder, scurried up both floors and got the hell out of Dodge. At the stairway door to the ninth floor, I paused long enough to brush the dust from the construction areas off my blouse and slacks. I went through the doorway on nine remembering my name badge backing at the last minute. I grabbed the elevator and ordered lunch when I got to the cafe in the lobby. I finished half a glass of water before my pulse rate returned to normal.

All through lunch I tried to figure out who I heard on the tenth floor. Had he…or she…followed me up there or were they there before me? Either way, my timing was lousy.

I pulled out my cell phone and dialed the number Dennis gave me. He was in a meeting but returned my call within ten minutes. I said, "I think you need to search the tenth floor here at the MAT building. I'm not sure you found everything."

"How would you know? Have you been sticking your nose where it doesn't belong…again?"

"I think people may be prowling around the crime scene on the tenth floor."

There was a long pause before Dennis spoke. "How would you know that?" He waited for me to respond, but I kept my mouth shut. "Casey? Are you still there?" I grunted a reply and he repeated himself. "How would you know? If you've been poking around where you don't belong, you could find yourself—"

"Just a hunch," I said.

"Yeah, right," he said. "Don't you know better? You could find yourself in deep trouble."

Yeah, right, I thought. That's not the impression Aaron picked up from you folks. Instead, I said, "And who would I be in trouble with?" You or the bad guys, I asked myself.

Dennis switched subjects and I wondered if he knew something I didn't. He asked me out for dinner tonight. "I've got something to do this evening, but I'm free tomorrow night." I always figure a counter offer is better than a turn down. My big evening was finding out what Effie learned today—if anything.

"Friday's fine. I think the Travelers are playing in town tomorrow night. Would you like to see a baseball game?"

"Sounds good to me." Not my immediate first choice for entertainment, but what the heck. I haven't seen a game in years. For a Texas League team, the Travelers do pretty well. I grew up in a Triple-A farm town and didn't have any sort of background for the major leaguers. I know the Travelers are an Angels' farm club, and I wracked my brain trying to remember what city the Angels play in these days. About thirty seconds was all I figured that knotty problem was worth, and I asked, "What time will you be by?"

"I'll pick you up about six at your place," he said. "We can grab hotdogs at the ballpark instead of dinner."

"Whoopee. That makes me a pretty cheap date."

"If you'd rather do something else…"

"I'm fine with it Dennis. You need to get used to my weird sense of humor or we're going to have problems."

14

I WAS ANXIOUS TO GET HOME TO SEE WHAT LUCK Effie had with her search. The afternoon crawled by, and I was early arriving at Cheryl's desk at break time. She grabbed her cordless phone and we were off to the lobby.

Seated at a small table with two lattes in front of us, I asked about the "extra" employees who seldom put in an appearance. She gave a furtive glance to both sides, leaned as far over the table as her ample bust would allow and whispered in a conspiratorial tone. Her conversation was punctuated on a regular basis with, "You know I don't like to gossip, but…" and "…remember, you didn't hear this from me."

I gave her a knowing nod each time she repeated the phrases accompanied by an occasional, "Of course." If she seemed to pause, I found a simple "And? …" prompted her to resume her story. I learned Cyber-Technology's business was in the dumper for months leading to the Year 2000 scare. Late in 1999, clients and appointments at the various businesses increased as C-T performed computer security checks.

"You know," Cheryl said, "I thought after January the first, two-thousand came and went, I might have to look for a new job. I figured with the scare over, Cyber-Technology would revert to their previous hardscrabble existence, but they surprised me."

I didn't even need to toss in an "and," a pair of raised eyebrows did the trick.

"Remember you didn't hear this from me. They didn't find many new customers, but the existing ones called more often. If the workload slowed down, Wayne would look at Mr.

Worthington and Mr. Eberheart and say, 'Time to do a main-frame Mambo.' I never understood what that was, but Mr. Worthington would kinda turn red and leave."

"How about Eberheart? Did he have the same reaction?"

"Naw. Nothing much fazes him. Sometimes I get the feeling he runs the place more than Wayne…I mean Mr. Harmon."

"I think you like the boss. Does he return the interest?" I gave her a big smile and the biggest stage wink I could muster.

Her face was turning as crimson as a setting sun. "Sort of…" she said. "But you didn't hear any of this from me."

I decided it was time to pull the office gossip train into the station and let it drop. Cheryl gave me more than she knew. The depot door was open and I knew we could get on board the same locomotive again.

The rest of the afternoon dragged. My brain felt like it was lugging a ball and chain along for the ride. I wanted to get away from the office, go home and discuss the day's results with my cohorts. I almost forgot to mention my parking arrangements to Wayne. I was on the way home when I remembered. I stuck my head in his door and gave him a quick run-down. He nodded and waved a backhand at me, which I took as a positive response. He put the phone up to his ear before I could say anything else. I left.

During the day, the storm front passed through Little Rock and was sneaking up on Mississippi to the east. I was looking forward to putting the Mustang's top down on the drive home. It would still be a bit muggy, but the wind whipping around the windshield would help. If worse came to worst, it wouldn't be the first time I cranked up the air conditioning with the top down. The car was a lucky buy. One of the few of "our" friends who didn't divorce me when Jarvis and I split offered it to me. He was a nut about cars and special ordered this one with a white top and six hand-rubbed coats of what he called "candy apple red" paint. He was moving up to a Porsche and he sold it to me for what seemed like a fortune, but in reality was an absolute steal. And, it was less than three years old.

I headed south to I-630 and swung west toward home. I kicked the Mustang hard enough it downshifted and accelerated up to the speed limit in seconds. When I pulled into my condo parking garage, I didn't bother with the top, hoping the next day would be another top-down day.

Effie was bustling around the kitchen humming to herself. Aaron walked in a few minutes later and we both went to our own rooms to shed our work clothes. I pulled an oversize T-shirt on over a sports bra and slipped into the same sweat shorts I wore the past few evenings. A pair of flip-flops completed my outfit and I checked myself in the full-length mirror. Oh, I thought. At-home chic.

Aaron was already in the kitchen when I came out. He was using a colander to rinse some lettuce and vegetables in the sink. I exercised my usual domestic expertise. I placed the napkins and silverware on the table in a flash. Effie didn't say a word as she coordinated her culinary ballet, so all her dishes arrived from the oven, fridge and counter at the same time. I assumed her quiet demeanor was a cover for a failure to gather any useful information today. If it was me and I could deliver good news, I would be gushing all over the place.

We sat at the table enjoying a tasty meatloaf, asparagus, biscuits and the salad Aaron created.

"I saw Dennis and his partner today," he said.

"I didn't know you were going to the police station before I leave."

"I'm on an overnight tomorrow and don't get back until Saturday, so I thought I'd take another run by them today."

I looked at him waiting for the next word. I waved my hands in a what's-up motion and he leaned back.

"Nothing new. They still seem to be fixated on the suicide theory. Dennis said he talked to you today."

"What did he say? Did he tell you what I told him?" I said.

"His partner walked up at that moment, and he clammed up pretty quick."

I told them about my conversation with Dennis. How he warned me off, saying I could get into trouble. "He keeps telling me to stay out of police business, but it's like there's a wink-wink, nudge-nudge at the same time."

"That's the feeling I keep getting from them," Aaron said. "Why the hell would they want an amateur messing around in their business?"

I didn't have an answer and it seemed, neither did Aaron. We let the question hang there in mid-air. Effie was silent all during dinner except a "thank you" when we complimented her on the meal. Too embarrassed by her failure today to say anything, I thought.

Effie looked up from her lap with a sly grin and said, "Is it my turn now?"

Aaron flashed a toothy smile and said, "You go, girl!"

I looked at the two of them grinning. I could have sworn there were canary feathers stuck in the corners of their mouths. "What's up with you two?"

"Effie did some great work today with the list of Cyber-Tech's clients you gave her." With that, Aaron got up, gave a low bow to Effie and said, "The floor is yours, milady." He began clearing the dishes from the table.

When Effie finished, I was flabbergasted. She not only talked to every company on the list, she developed contacts, which would fit the loose-lips-sink-ships category. Opinion revision time again, I told myself. Every time I make an assumption about Effie, she pulls another rabbit out. I was beginning to wonder who was Eliza and who was Professor Higgins.

The expression on my face must have been a give-away. Aaron stared at me from the sink and said, "She's a real pisser, ain't she?"

Effie began to turn red and I laughed. "I don't know I would have chosen those exact words, but you are a most amazing and talented young lady." She got redder.

Effie told us everyone on the list became a client of Cyber-Technology in the last few months of 1999. C-T worked in all the offices updating their computer security and looking for holes in their software, which might allow an outsider to penetrate their computer systems. They were allowed to open an email account at each company so "they could exchange information with CT's main office." They were given free rein to change any hardware and software considered a security threat.

"I learned about a couple of companies who weren't on your list, Casey," Effie said. "I confirmed them from more than one of my sources. I guess they balked at giving C-T so much power over their systems." She handed me a list and said, "I bet if you check old files, you'll find them."

Effie produced reams of detail about each client—what they bought and how much they paid to Cyber-Technology. "Of course, these are estimates. My contacts didn't have time to check details. They did it off the top of their heads."

C-T made a ton of money during that period, and they picked up a great deal of repeat business from each client in 2000 and since. When these companies developed a computer problem, they asked Cyber-Technology to do follow-up work. She showed us the approximate dates for the reported problems.

I told them I would crosscheck with Cheryl to see if any of these dates coincided with Wayne Harmon's joke about a mainframe dance. They asked me what I meant. "I think C-T has a way to sabotage their clients' computers. I'd hate to cause trouble for anyone like Cheryl who's innocent, but…I'm afraid there are more guilty than innocent. I think I'll see if I can break into a client computer from here."

Aaron and Effie were both ready to participate in the experiment. I told them we'd wait until Saturday night—late—when there's less chance of being noticed. I looked at Effie and said, "How in the world did you get all this information?"

"I called pretending I worked for the state. I didn't say which state and I created a Department of Computer Security and Millennium Follow Up. It's amazing how people want to help when I told them I was interested in what sort of problems they encountered before and after the Year 2000 scare."

"You did all this on a lunch hour and coffee breaks?" I said.

"It was pretty slow today, so I made a couple of calls during regular hours."

Lights flashed and police sirens sounded in my head. "I hope you didn't use the phones at your work. The police could trace the calls back and find you. Tell me you at least used a pay phone."

Effie shook her head. "I thought about that, so I decided to use one of those throw-away cell phones. No one can trace them."

Aaron and I both sat there with our mouths hanging open—speechless.

I thought about where we were and what we were doing. "Look, you two; I got wrapped up in this case when I first decided the deaths were murders. I also got mad at Dennis because he and the police didn't seem to be interested in the deaths. That's okay for me, but I don't think I ever gave you two a choice about being involved. I just assumed you would follow my lead. Now, I need to give you the opportunity go your own way and pull out of all of this."

I looked at Effie and Aaron, and I couldn't decide if their expressions were positive or negative —

"I've got no problems being part of the investigation," Aaron said.

Effie looked at me with wide eyes. "This is the most exciting thing I've ever done in my life. There is no way you're going to leave me behind."

I breathed a sigh of relief. I knew I could count on these two who have become friends.

15

FRIDAY MORNING DAWNED BRIGHT AND WARM. THE rains of the previous day did little to ameliorate the temperature. The computerized thermometer on the dash read 75, and the ride to work with the top down was bearable. The weatherman predicted high 90s today and humidity as high as well, the heat index promised to be around 105. I was glad to have an underground parking spot. I put the top up, armed the car's security system and went up to Cyber-Technology's offices.

I stopped at Cheryl's reception desk long enough to confirm a latte break with her this morning. I wanted as much information as I could gather for my weekend computer foray.

During the morning, I decrypted more email stored on C-T's server. They were grouped into folders by client name. Not all the messages were encoded. The plain text ones seemed to be routine correspondence between a C-T tech on-site at a client's place of business and C-T staff here in the office. I spent the bulk of my time on the encoded ones. I selected the accounting firm, Boneventure, Smith & Carsten, LLC…the one Brian Hawkins, the first body in the lobby, worked for. I ran one of their emails through my handy dandy code-breaking software and found cryptic information inside. It began with the two words: tropical sojourner and then listed a string of numbers. I noticed the first three repeated at regular intervals. Parsing the list based on the repeats, they were seven digits long. Ah ha—phone numbers. There were five sets of numbers in the list, but the phone book showed a single number for the firm.

I called Effie and described the situation and wondered aloud about the extra four lines.

"I'll call you back in fifteen minutes," she said.

True to her word, I was talking to Effie again in less than a quarter-hour. She discovered two lines were rollovers for the main number, the next one in order belonged to the head of the firm, Mr. Boneventure, and was a private line. The fifth one was reserved for their employees so they could access the company's computer while they were at home or on the road.

"Great," I said. "Now I know how to get to their mainframe. Who were you this time, to get all this information?"

"Don't ask," Effie said.

* * *

There was enough time, but none to spare, for me to get home and change clothes before Dennis picked me up. I wondered what one should wear to a baseball game. A pair of blue, medium length shorts, a matching tank top and sandals seemed to be a good choice. At the last minute, I grabbed one of my larger purses. It would accommodate a wrap-around skirt and a lightweight, powder blue sweater. Just in case Dennis wants to stop somewhere after the game, I thought.

I met him in the lobby and he helped me into his car. It was several years old, and I wouldn't have recognized the make if the blue oval with four cursive letters in it wasn't so obvious. The car was so filthy on the outside I hesitated to get in. Fortunately, the interior was a lot cleaner. When we hit the freeway into town, the dusty old coupe surprised me. "Is the engine stock?"

Dennis grinned and shook his head. "I've got a siren and flashing lights in the grill."

We made excellent time to Ray Winder Field. The trip couldn't have been much shorter even if Dennis ran Code Three. At the ticket window, he said, "Do you like to be close? I can get us box seats." When I shrugged, he said, "Two, General Admission," to the ticket lady. He turned to me and said, "I like to be up a bit. I think you get a better view."

Since he paid for us to get in, I popped for dinner. Two hot dogs and two beers were more reasonable than I anticipated. I got more change back from a twenty than I expected. We settled into a pair of seats about fifteen rows up. Straight out in front of me was home plate with the base lines diverging out toward the walls. I took a good pull on my beer when we were enveloped in a fog. Three rows down and a little to our left sat a large man chomping on a cigar and loosing great clouds of smoke. He was enormous, but he wasn't tall—he was obese. I nudged Dennis and wrinkled my nose. The foul-line flags indicated a slight breeze blowing in from left field. I nodded my head that direction and we moved to another pair of seats putting Huge-O downwind from us. Now we could enjoy the aroma of roasted peanuts and popcorn floating on the air rather than choking cigar smoke. We propped our feet up on the empty seats in front of us, munched our hot dogs and chugged beer as the announcer read the starting line-ups over the public address system.

We were in the bottom half of the first inning when my curiosity overrode any interest in sports. "What the hell is going on with the deaths in the building where I work?" Dennis pretended not to hear me, so I dug an elbow into his bicep.

"I heard you," he said, massaging his arm. "I was trying to think of a good answer."

"Are you aware there are crude construction ladders leading through holes in the concrete floor from the twelfth floor down to ten?"

"Yes. But how would you know about them? Those floors are off-limits, they're a crime scene."

"Crime scene? How come you aren't investigating?"

"Who says we aren't?"

I banged my fist down on the armrest between our seats. "Damnit. You know I'm nosing around the building. You warn me about trouble. A friend says you're stuck on the suicide angle but is betting you don't want me to stop my busy-body routine."

"A friend?…Oh, you must mean Aaron." I nodded and he continued. "We don't have a shred of physical evidence pointing to murder. We don't have anyone with a motive. If it is murder, I'm hoping you pick up on something resembling a reason why those two guys are dead."

He twisted in his seat, looked at me and said, "Be careful. If someone killed either of the two, they won't take kindly to someone poking around in their business."

"I've stumbled onto something, but I don't think it has anything to do with the killings."

"What?"

"I'll know more later. Maybe Monday."

Dennis frowned but didn't press the issue and we both settled into our seats to watch the game. By the third inning, the Travelers were one run down, but there were men on base. There was a crack of the bat against horsehide as the batter connected with the next pitch. We hooted and cheered as a pair of Travs crossed the plate and they were one up. At the seventh inning stretch, we stood and I swung my arms to loosen the muscles. I turned toward one of the exits and took a step.

Dennis put a hand on my arm and said, "Where are we going?"

I needed a restroom, but guessed he was talking about us as a couple. I liked him, but after Jarvis the Rat I wasn't sure I could trust another man with my feelings. I did my best to explain to Dennis, but my rambling was a way to grope for an escape hatch.

Dennis moved his hand up to my shoulder. "Casey, I care about you and would like our relationship to continue. If all it can be for now is an occasional date, I'll accept that to give us a chance."

I wanted more, and was afraid to say it. I took his hand and we sat down to watch the bottom of the seventh.

16

I SPENT MOST OF SATURDAY READING AND THINKING about last night. I like Dennis and hoped he would be willing to go at a snail's pace with our relationship. I bored myself and decided to do some light house cleaning. Every time I picked up a dust cloth, Effie wrestled it away from me as she said, "Let me do it." I took a couple of steps toward the closet where I keep the hose for the central vacuum system and she was on me again.

"Okay, okay," I said. "I'll go back to reading."

Aaron arrived home in late afternoon. We decided on Chinese and ordered in. By seven p.m., we finished off the food, rinsed the white containers and cleaned the kitchen.

"How long before we do our hacker bit?" Effie said.

Aaron nodded in agreement and seemed to reflect the same enthusiasm.

I led the way to the den with PK following close behind. Sitting down, I jiggled the mouse to wake the computer from its power-saving nap. PK assumed his favorite perch during computer time. He leaped up on top of the monitor and lay down. He wouldn't move until we were finished. Clicking on the modem icon, I typed Boneventure's phone number into the box, and clicked the OK button. The screen changed, showing the company's initials B,S&C LLC and two text input boxes. The first one was labeled USER ID. Now what? I typed in the letters CT thinking it was as good a guess as any and moved to the second box, which asked for a password. I knew it and said, "No sweat." I typed, "tropical sojourner" and hit the Enter key. The screen read INVALID PASSWORD and reverted back to its original configuration—two blank boxes.

"Why didn't the password work?" Effie said.

I was wracking my brain. Maybe it's case sensitive. I typed "Tropical Sojourner" and tried Enter once more. INVALID PASSWORD stared back at me, again. "I hate smart-ass computers." I tried to guess the number of combinations of upper and lower case letters in a password seventeen characters long. My mind ground to a halt. Then I remembered a trick I used on a previous occasion. "If this doesn't work, we may be screwed for now. A lot of systems toss you out after three failed attempts." I hit the CAPS LOCK key and typed "tROPICAL sOJOURNER" into the second blank. This time when I hit the Enter key, the picture dissolved and we were looking at a screen reading: Boneventure, Smith & Carsten, LLC - MENU.

"Hot damn," I said. "We're in!" I glanced at Effie and Aaron who sat in chairs pulled up on either side of me. I leaned back to bask in the glory of my hacker skills.

My basking was short lived. Effie was rubbing her hands together and Aaron said, "What's next, Oh, Fearless Leader?"

Below the word "Menu" was a list of categories. Several caught my eye: Accounts Payable, Accounts Receivable, Client List, Online Tax Reference, and Audits in Progress.

We pawed our way through all the areas displayed on the menu. The two financial categories were boring. The client list included a number of private corporations and we reviewed their balance sheets and operating statements. Other than being able to tiptoe through sensitive financial data, none of us could see anything of value to Cyber-Technology. We skipped the Online Tax Reference item and found the Audits in Progress another mind-numbing area.

"Go back to the Client List," Effie said.

As I did, she pulled out the hand-written C-T client list I gave her earlier. She held the paper up next to the screen so all three of us could view it.

"See," she said. "At least six or more of the accounting firm's clients are also clients of C-T."

Aaron and I both responded with blank stares, so Effie expanded her theory. "If they can't profit directly from a company—except to do some work on their computer—they tap the client list and go after them as clients for C-T."

Aaron leaned forward and stared at the list on the computer screen. "There must be other ways. Just signing up clients doesn't guarantee work for C-T."

"I think they create their own business," I said. "I bet when they went into these companies during the Millennium scare, they left a back door open for themselves on each client computer system."

"So, what's a back door?" Aaron said.

Before I could answer, Effie jumped in. "It's a term for a programmer's way of slipping past the security on a network of computers."

"How'd you know that?" Aaron said.

"I read a lot."

"She's right on," I said. "I think we've already used part of the opening. We used the password C-T left in the Boneventure's system. They do their dirty work at the Administrator's level. That means they can not only create problems on a network, they also know where to go to fix the glitch—after billing hours and hours of doing nothing."

Effie asked if I could log onto the system as the Administrator. I tried the few commands I could remember and discovered my memory was failing me. "Never fear," I said. "I know someone who can."

I dialed a young man I know. When he answered, I used his internet handle, CrackerJack. He prefers to be called a "cracker." Hackers have become too destructive for his tastes. I explained my situation at C-T and asked if he could help. From the tone of his voice, I could almost see him rubbing his hands together and muttering under his breath, "Let me at 'em." He asked for my IP address, which I gave him. In a few seconds, my computer screen began to dance without me touching the keyboard. "He's logged onto my computer and is controlling it from his machine," I said.

I knew by now CrackerJack was wearing a headset with a boom mike. With that equipment, he could talk on the phone and maintain a typing pace rivaling a machine gun. I told him a pair of cohorts were watching and asked his permission to put him on the speakerphone. The three of us listened to a rapid-fire narration that matched his typing speed.

CrackerJack explained the steps and access he achieved. He told me my guesses were accurate and said, "Would you like me to leave a little time bomb in here? That way you could see how good those folks at Cyber-Technology really are at problem solving."

I thought about it for a minute. "Okay, but don't do anything to damage the computers…or cost them money in case they track this back to me."

"Don't worry, Casey," the voice from the speakerphone said. "I modified the file tracking log-ins and your computer's address is nowhere in sight."

He gave me instructions about how to log out without leaving a trail of breadcrumbs. "This was fun. If you need any more crack-ins, give me a shout."

"Thanks, CrackerJack," I said. "We may have more fun evenings to share."

17

SUNDAY MORNING DAWNED WITH A CLOUDY SKY. BY the time the plates that held Belgium waffles were washed, the sky displayed only a few puffy white clouds.

Effie, Aaron and I sat in the living room enjoying the view and pretending the Sunday edition of the paper was holding our attention. I knew I felt that way and I caught the other two eyeing me over the top of a folded section of newspaper.

Almost as if on cue, each of us tossed aside the papers we were holding, stared at one another and burst into conversation.

"Wow—"

"Last night—"

"Did we—do that?"

"Are you sure—can't—track—"

The volume of our voices increased as we sought to be the center of this disjointed rant. We repeated each other's words until Aaron and I were standing and shouting.

Aaron threw both arms up in the air and yelled, "Whoa."

We collapsed back into our seats convulsed with laughter.

"Maybe we should draw straws to see who goes first," I said. Another round of laughing.

Aaron leaned forward looking at Effie and me to see if we wanted to speak. Since we were quiet, he began. "Casey, I wonder if you're ascribing too many sinister motives to C-T's actions. Do you really think they're involved in criminal activity?"

"What do you have to say, Effie?" I said.

"First, this is the most exciting thing I've ever done." She rose, walked to the window and stared out for a moment. Turning back toward us she said, "I think Cyber-Technology is up to something. If it's not downright illegal, it's at least unethical. What else can you call it—leaving a way for them to invade the computers in their clients' offices."

I listened to her. Not only her words, but also her voice. In under two weeks, she eased most of the Arkansan out of her words—especially when she wanted to communicate a serious thought. "Effie," I said, "don't ever lose all your accent. It's you— it's part of your charm."

Aaron nodded in agreement and Effie soaked up the compliment like a spring flower drinks in the rain.

I looked at Aaron and said, "I agree with Effie's position. If we can find enough to make a case of C-T breaking the law, we'll go to the cops. If it's a matter of ethics, I can always turn CrackerJack loose on them."

* * *

On Monday morning, the three of us were off to work. Aaron would be gone for the day on an out-and-back and I dropped Effie at her office building. I used the time it took Effie to exit the car to put the top down. I figured I might as well enjoy the morning. The weather guy on TV was forecasting uncomfortable temperatures and humidity for the drive time this evening.

Cyber-Tech made no effort to replace Ross Worthington after his swan dive from the tenth floor, so I eased the Mustang into his reserved parking slot.

Instead of taking the elevator to the ninth floor, I walked up to the lobby. I entered the atrium area and stopped. I was looking for something that would make sense of two men dying here on the marble floor.

Staring straight ahead from the door I entered, I faced the street-side entrance. These two entrances were on the short sides of the huge oval atrium. The wall behind me and the one I faced were gigantic expanses of glass up to the top floor. To my right and left were the matching towers of office space. They occupied the long sides of the atrium.

Tower B—the East Tower—where I worked was on my left— Tower A on my right. The twins faced each other like a pair of giants in a staring contest.

I moved to the center of the lobby floor and turned three hundred and sixty degrees taking in the details. Each floor above the lobby sported a balcony encircling the open area. Even from this vantage point, the top three floors, ten, eleven and twelve, gave an unfinished look. I crossed to a spot near where the first body landed. I wondered why Brian Hawkins from the accounting firm on the eighth floor went up to ten.

I took a deep breath and closed my eyes. Today, after two weeks, I could still hear the sickening sound of his body hitting the floor. The sickening smell of his blood spreading across the tiles still assaulted my nostrils. I could identify the spot where the janitorial staff failed to remove the last trace of the stain. A shiver ran up my spine and I decided I'd spent enough time gawking for now.

I whistled through my work for the morning. That's a euphemism—I never learned to whistle, and it drove my brother nuts. He would spend what seemed like hours demonstrating how to pucker my lips and whistle. I like thinking of Jason, but it's painful. I was looking forward to entering kindergarten in the fall when the word came in the middle of the summer. My brother, almost fourteen years older than me, was dead—killed in Vietnam.

I hurried to the ninth floor restroom to repair my makeup. I was sure the tears welling up as I thought of my brother streaked my cheeks with mascara. I was right.

Returning from the makeup repair, I was about to turn a hallway corner in the C-T office, when I heard voices. Wayne Harmon said, "…are you sure there's nothing up there?"

It took a second to place the other person. Winston Eberheart said, "Seems like every time I've been up there, I heard someone else. I tried to locate them, but no luck."

By the sound of their voices, I could tell they were getting closer. Their conversation ceased when they turned the corner and saw me. "Hi, there," I said and breezed by them on the way to my cubicle.

Later, when I glanced at the clock, I was delighted to see the hands pointing at—coffee break. I needed to continue the internal dialogue I began first thing this morning. I could have used some time at my desk to do that, but I do my best to give an employer one hundred percent for the paycheck they give me.

I decided the coffee shop would offer a good spot to continue my snooping activity. Sipping coffee, I leaned back and looked toward the top three floors. The coffee shop was on the opposite side of the atrium from where the two guys fell to their deaths. I was absorbed in my thoughts when a voice startled me.

"Hi! Mind if I join you?"

It was Cheryl from my office.

"What were you staring at up there?"

"I was thinking about Ross Worthington and the other guy who fell. Have you heard anything about them?…About why they fell?"

Cheryl leaned forward with a hand cupped around her mouth. She surprised me because the first words were not: You didn't hear this from me.

"As a matter of fact, there's been some rumors. I heard the cops are looking for someone who's been prowling around them construction floors."

She looked at her watch. "Oh, Lordy. I gotta get back. Spent too much time in the gift shop."

In a whoosh, I was alone again. This time, when I looked at the top floors, I could still hear Wayne and Winston Eberheart referring to "up there." Any number of C-T's clients were located in tall buildings, even a couple in the Metropolitan Bank building. They could be thought of as "up there." We also had clients in North Little Rock who could be considered "up there." I continued to stare upward and a peculiar feeling in my stomach said—the tenth floor is "up there." Even Cheryl used those same words to describe the top floors. I called Dennis when I got back to my office to ask him to come by the MAT building. He was busy, but said he could see me at two-thirty.

* * *

The clock over the coffee shop's back counter was one of those Felix-the-Cat characters. As his eyes flipped side to side, he seemed to say, "Dennis is late. Dennis is late." The clock hands confirmed he was running twenty minutes behind schedule.

I was working on a zinger of a greeting when a voice whispered in my ear, "Good detectives never let anyone sneak up behind them."

Instead of a caustic comment, I concentrated all my energy in regaining my composure. The best I could do was, "Dennis Epstein, you're a sneaky shit."

The Grand Canyon grin on his face was infectious. Any anger I had for his late arrival faded and I found myself picturing us naked in my bed.

"Casey, you look flushed. Are you coming down with something?"

In my mind, I put my clothes back on and reached out to the clothed hunk sitting across from me. "I'm fine. What's new with the investigation?"

Dennis "ran the case," explaining to me that was how he brought his superiors up to date on an inquiry. It boiled down to: two dead, no motives, most likely two suicides.

"I still don't believe those men took their own lives," I said. "Several times when I've been up on the construction floors, I heard someone."

He was scowling, but said, "Did you get a look at anyone?"

"No. I hauled ass when I heard the noise." I told him about the "up there" reference I heard from Winston Eberheart.

"That's a pretty thin stretch. Hardly probable cause for anything."

"Didn't think you needed cause to search the tenth floor again. It's still a potential crime scene, isn't it?"

Dennis nodded an agreement and I told him about what I saw up there. Some sort of foreign material on the underside of the metal railing.

"If you've tampered with evidence, you could be in trouble and whatever's there could be tainted."

"I've never been anywhere, but if you got an anonymous tip, you'd investigate, wouldn't you?"

"Okay. What would this anonymous tipster tell us to look for?"

I asked if the shoe Hawkins was wearing, the one that fell by itself, was scuffed. Dennis was quiet for a moment and then said he thought he remembered seeing a comment to that effect in the reports. I described in detail what I saw and where it was.

"I'll get the Crime Scene Search Unit folks to take another look," he said.

He stood, leaned over and kissed me on the cheek. He was gone before I could say a word. The picture in my head flipped back to the earlier version of him in my bed.

18

LAST NIGHT—NO CALL FROM DENNIS. THIS MORNING I finished an entire days' work before my morning break. Still no call. Lunch in the atrium cafe. No call, and I'm going nuts waiting. Afternoon—in the lobby again sipping a latte—still waiting.

I looked up and movement caught my eye. From my angle of view, I had trouble making out the person. Looked like someone wearing green boots with ghost-white hands. A second figure appeared. Same strange garb. Crime scene investigators, I said to myself. Then I looked around at my fellow coffee sippers to determine if I uttered those words aloud. No one staring at me, so I guess I'm safe.

I moved to another table for a better view. I still couldn't see much, so I headed for the elevators where I exited on nine. I hurried into the stairwell and up to twelve, stepping over the yellow tape stretched across the doorway.

I moved to a point where I could see across the open atrium area and look down on the tenth floor. My hand rummaged through my purse and closed on the small binoculars. They were better than nothing, but didn't put me up close enough to make out much detail. I could see a camera resting atop a short stack of construction material. There appeared to be some paper and plastic bags lying near the camera. A man and a woman were crouched near the railing. The man moved to one end of the open area and lay down on the concrete peering at the bottom of the railing. He inched forward. Near the center, he stopped and spoke to his partner. She handed him a small instrument. The man plucked something from under the metal railing and placed it in the plastic bag she held out toward him.

Hot damn! I said to myself. I think they found it. At least it's near the spot I described to Dennis. I let out a long sigh of satisfaction.

I hurried back to my office on nine assuming Dennis would call shortly. At four forty-five, I gave up waiting. I left a message with the Desk Sergeant at the police department on West Markham Street. I also left a reminder that he could get me on my cell phone as well. I left my cell number on his voice mail and his pager.

* * *

I ranted through supper. Aaron and Effie remained silent, having learned it was useless trying to talk to me at a time like that. With my mouth moving at a rate of a thousand words per minute with gusts up to fifteen hundred, it was impossible for an outsider to engage my mind. I was too busy listening to myself.

By dessert, I slowed to a more conversational speed. Aaron looked at me and said, "I think you're taking this whole thing too seriously. This isn't the only case the police are working. You can't expect them to drop everything else and return your calls."

I shrugged and shook my head.

"Why aren't we doing more computer snooping?" Effie said.

"I'm too wrapped up in the murders," I said, biting each word and spitting it out.

Effie gave me her wide-eyed, angelic smile and said, "All the more reason to do something to take your mind off them…and Dennis not calling you back."

I was approaching the point where I couldn't argue with her logic. Effie could disarm me with her smile, and sneak up on me and whack me in the side of the head with a figurative two-by-four as the attention-getting step. So much for trying to do anything more for my Eliza Doolittle, I thought. I better pay attention to her and learn.

Looking at Effie I said, "I'll get more company email in the morning. We can do some hacking tomorrow night." I picked up the cordless, went into my room and shut the door. The answering machine at Dennis' home completed its spiel and I heard the beep. "Damnit, Dennis are you home?" How could he not respond to such a delightful opening, I thought, and tried to reel in my emotions. "I'm sorry, Dennis. If you are home, please pick up."

"Hi," came the reply. "Sorry, Casey but I was getting out of the shower. Damn near killed myself getting to the phone."

I pictured him, towel wrapped around his trim waist racing into his bedroom. My imagination ran wild. About half-way there, the towel fell away and dropped to the floor. Now he was standing there, naked, talking to me.

"Casey…Casey, are you still there?"

I jerked myself part way out of my fantasy. "Yes" was all I could muster. I was still imagining him without clothes. "Yes. Did your crime scene folks find anything?"

"And, how would you know the CSSU team was out today… anywhere?"

"Just a hunch."

"Aw, bullshit, Casey. You're not quite as clever as you think you are. I told them not to get too excited if they saw someone snooping on them. They spotted you."

"I'm in my bedroom getting ready to go to sleep." I looked at the bedside clock, which read, eight-fifteen. No way he'll believe me…I wonder if he's picturing me in the buff.

"Casey, what in the world are you talking about? You asked a question. Do you want an answer?"

In my daydream, he was thinking about me naked on the bed. He was interested…without the towel it was obvious.

"Hello. Earth to Casey. Are you still there?"

My image of him vanished. "Okay. What?"

"I think we found something. Won't be sure till tomorrow, and—"

"What? What did you find?"

"Wouldn't be good to discuss details on the phone. Could I stop by day after tomorrow, and see you at work?"

"Ah…yeah. Friday is okay." I reminded him what time I planned to take my break and that I'd meet him in the lobby. We hung up and I lay back on the bed and closed my eyes. I did my best to revive my image of Dennis…sans towel. No luck, so I got up and went back to the living room. I briefed my cohorts on the call and knew I would have a tough time sleeping this evening and the next night—for more than one reason.

19

THE THURSDAY MAIL AT CYBER-TECHNOLOGY WAS heavier than usual. Even with that load, there wasn't enough to keep me busy long. I reflected on how slow time moves when my mind is idle. I wondered how the regular gal, Celia, kept from going nuts on this job. She was either from a shallow gene pool or she brought her knitting along from home.

I dug into C-T's server and transferred some email and client files onto my thumb drives. When I finished, there were two of the small USB drives filled with surreptitiously garnered information in my purse. That should keep us busy tonight, I thought.

* * *

My co-conspirators joined me around the dinner table at home. Aaron, Effie and I talked about the murders and found ourselves whispering. After several exchanges in hushed tones, we looked at one another and fell silent. Then, we all burst out laughing.

After dinner, we left the table at the same time. PK must have assumed we were headed to the den and the computer. By the time we arrived there, he was already snoozing on top of the monitor.

We spent about an hour looking at the servers of Austin Consultants, a professional engineering firm, and Ouachita Financial Planners. The Austin computer contained an unprotected area in which all of their project bids were displayed.

"Now there's something that could be worth money," Aaron said. Between Effie and me, he got four raised eyebrows, so he continued, "If Austin is bidding on a job, what would the amount of their bid be worth to competitors for that same business?"

I logged off the Austin Consultants' computer and entered the address for the one at Cyber-Technology. We located email between C-T and another engineering firm. Although the messages didn't spell it out, it looked like CT was selling bid information about "AC" to a third company. "AC could only mean Austin Consultants," I said.

Before we could add that to our murder conspiracies, the phone rang. I listened and then said, "CrackerJack, good to hear from you. Thanks for checking your inbox; you're right on time. I'm putting you on speakerphone. Effie and Aaron are here too."

He got right to business. "What do you want to do, Casey?"

"I want to do something to the computers at the Bonaventure Accounting firm in the MAT building. Nothing destructive, maybe a major inconvenience. It should happen this weekend, and I need a clue to the fix so I can feed it to Boneventure's secretary. Then she'll owe me. I need to pump her about people in her office."

"You got it." CrackerJack fell silent, but we could hear the activity on his keyboard. Fifteen minutes of steady typing and he said, "Done."

He briefed me on the glitch he'd introduced to the Boneventure computer, but most of it went over my head. Eye rolls and head shakes told me Aaron and Effie were also in the dark. CrackerJack gave me the "clue" to pass on to the secretary and said, "It's generic enough she won't have to be a computer geek to have heard of it and it'll be enough for her computer guys to run with and solve the problem."

I told CrackerJack I'd been snooping on other computers tonight. "Did you wipe out your footprints before you left?" he said.

I gulped and said, "No. I forgot. Am I busted?"

"As late in the evening as it is, I doubt it. Give me the names and I'll cover you. Gal, you ain't never gonna be a decent cracker if you don't attend to the details."

I gave him the addresses and passwords for Austin, Ouachita and C-T.

CrackerJack laughed and said, "I got your back, Casey," and hung up.

20

I AWOKE AROUND FOUR IN THE MORNING. IT WAS already getting light outside and Friday promised to be a less than decent day—weather-wise that is. I wasn't sure about the rest. The previous night we found the information on Cyber-Technology's computer proving they were hacking into the servers of their clients. I wasn't sure how well I could look them in the eye at the office and not give away my suspicions. Sometimes I'm good at that and sometimes…

I staggered out of bed and stumbled toward the bathroom. I'm not the fleetest of foot at that hour of the morning. About half-way across the room, the door inched open.

A smiling face peered in at me. Effie said, "What would you like for breakfast today?"

My tongue went on a short expedition. "Please don't even mention food until I've scrubbed my mouth with a toothbrush."

Effie sat on the edge of my bed as I reached for my bathroom utensils. I managed to squeeze a lump of toothpaste onto the brush with minimal spillage into the sink. We talked about the events of last night. Effie did most of the talking. I gurgled responses as I ran the brush over my teeth. We were positive C-T was stealing from clients and wondered out loud if that could be tied in any way to the deaths at the MAT building. I rinsed my mouth, raised my head and looked in the mirror. Behind me was the unit I call the over-the-John storage cabinet. It hangs on the wall about two feet above the toilet water tank with a shelf at the bottom and two doors above that. It isn't tall enough to make it to the ceiling, so there is about a foot of space at the top.

There he sat—PK—up on top striking the pose where he looks like Snoopy imitating a vulture. "PK, get down from there." The authoritative tone of my voice failed. PK lay down and rolled over and over, keeping at least one eye on me the entire time.

"What did you say, Casey?" came from my bedroom.

I invited Effie in to see old Psycho Kitty and we continued our discussion. There was still no evidence tying C-T's fraud to the murders.

At the breakfast table, we updated Aaron on our latest ideas. He didn't add anything and I wondered if he was as frustrated as I was.

Aaron was off for the day and I told Effie I would drop her on my way to town. It was going to be another high-humidity scorcher today.

* * *

Dennis caught me by the arm as I emerged from the parking garage elevator at the MAT building. "I have a meeting I can't duck. Need to take off right now. Should be able to get back here by eleven. Can we have an early lunch?"

I got in a quick nod before he took off at a trot toward the street exit. He never looked back, so he missed the fist I shook at him.

Rather than doing my work, I spent the morning drinking coffee in the break room, which is, so not me. I chalked it up to the stress of the past few days. Several times Cheryl came by and we talked. No news from the building grapevine. I asked her if she knew of any link between Hawkins from the accounting firm downstairs and Ross Worthington. "I mean, did they ever work together when C-T was troubleshooting their computers?"

Cheryl said, "I suppose so, but I don't remember anything specific…Ah…Do you think it's connected? I mean, are the two deaths related?"

"I doubt it. I was just wondering."

The hands on the clock were frozen. Seemed to me, the only thing that could move slower was a dead snail. By ten-thirty I gave up and made my way to the lobby. Maybe, please maybe, Dennis'll be early. He wasn't. It was eleven-twenty when I saw him come through the door from the underground garage.

We got into the cafeteria-style line and I moved behind him. "Are you going to pay?" he said.

"No. You're paying. I'm back here to shove you through the line faster."

When we sat down at a table, he reached for a fork. "No you don't," I said grabbing his arm. "No eating until you tell me what your crime scene folks found."

"We've gotten the biggest break so far in the case." He paused and looked at me.

I was eating, but I stuck an index finger up in the air and waved it around in a small circle. "Keep on talking. I'll let you know when you can start eating."

"The Crime Scene Techs found a bit of leather on the bottom edge of the metal railing up there on the tenth floor. I knew that two days ago—"

My fork stopped in mid-air. "Then why the hell didn't you tell me then?"

"Because it meant nothing then. Today, the lab boys tell us it came from the loafer Brian Hawkins was wearing the day he went over the ledge. They can match it to a scuffed spot on his shoe—the one, which landed in the planter."

"The one I told you hit after the body did?" I said.

"Yep. No doubt about it now. Hawkins went over the railing and his shoe was kicked or pushed under the railing afterwards."

"Then it's murder, isn't it?"

"Yep, again. Casey, you have to keep this quiet. My job is on the line if it gets out I've been sharing this evidence with you."

"But I'm the one who told you where to look."

"I know, but even that could get me in trouble. Even with what we've found, we don't have a case against anyone. All we have is probable cause it was murder. We don't have any suspects, let alone a motive."

I told him I thought we might have motive with the fraud I uncovered. Dennis said it was worth looking at, but it still wasn't strong enough to tie it all together. He said, "If the deaths are murder, how do they tie to the fraud?"

I waved a hand at him and told him it was okay to eat. He dug into his plate of spaghetti, then reached for a packet of parmesan. Since I was finished with my meal, I sat back and watched him. My thoughts went back two nights and I pictured him in his bedroom with the towel around his ankles. The image stirred my mind. My mind stirred my body and my body was stirring. I crossed my legs and tore my gaze away from him.

He finished his food and we talked for a few more minutes. The second death still didn't make any sense and there seemed to be no motive for it either. By twelve-oh-five, he was saying his goodbyes. "Remember, keep your eyes and ears open."

I watched him leave and went back to the ninth floor. The rest of the afternoon went by somewhere near the speed of light.

21

SATURDAY MORNING OVER BREAKFAST, I TOLD EFFIE and Aaron about my meeting with Dennis the day before. "The police have evidence indicating there were suspicious circumstances about the first death." They wanted to know the details, but I promised Dennis I wouldn't discuss the actual evidence with anyone. "I can't tell you that, but the police believe my first eyewitness report."

"Do they think it was a murder?" Effie said.

"That's about the size of it."

Aaron leaned toward us and said, "How about the second death? Was it a murder too?"

We spent the next hour hashing out the details of both deaths. We couldn't put a motive to either and weren't sure they were even related. "Dennis wants me to keep snooping around the MAT building."

"That doesn't sound like a good idea," Aaron said. "I mean, what if the murderer gets wind of what you're doing. Wouldn't you be in danger?"

"I don't think there'll be a problem. I'll be careful and with any luck no one will even know I'm looking for more evidence."

About mid-morning, I put in a call to CrackerJack. I got a connection, but he was quiet for a long time. I could hear him typing in the background. When he did respond, I told him I needed another favor.

"Is it life or death, Babe?" I told him no, and he said, "I'm tied up in a project right now. Could keep me busy for several days. Tell you what. Give me another call on Wednesday and I promise I'll help you then. Hey, the little time bomb I left for the accounting folks should be going off right about now."

The next sound I heard was a dial tone. I hung up and the three of us continued talking about The Case of the Plunging Bodies, the name Effie selected for our whodunit. "Let's take the sequence of the murders," I said. "Hawkins from Boneventure Accounting dies first and Worthington from my office is killed to cover the first one or to confuse the issue."

Effie said, "And what if Hawkins was killed to cover the fact Mr. Worthington was the real victim?"

"There's a third possibility," Aaron said. "What if the two murders are not related?…Wait a minute. Casey, you said the police think the first one was murder, but they have nothing on the second one. Right?" I nodded and he continued, "Okay, then what if the second one was a real suicide?"

"Good grief," Effie said. "Now we've got four possible scenarios. We're no better off than before."

"We're in worse shape," I added. "I need to do some deep digging at Cyber-Technology this coming week."

We spent most of the balance of the weekend doing our best imitation of veggies and couch potatoes.

* * *

The weekend over, I was anxious to see if the computer glitch CrackerJack left on the Boneventure computers was rearing its ugly head. Cheryl and I were sipping coffee in the break room when our boss, Wayne Harmon, came in with Winston Eberheart. Wayne was telling about the three calls on his voice mail from Boneventure.

Eberheart said, "To hell with them. They're nothing but a bunch of crybabies. I'll go down there this afternoon. I've got other things I want to do this morning."

Wow, I thought. That's a delightful way to treat clients. I

grinned on the inside at his attitude. It would give me all morning to talk to their secretary, Janet Wilson. If Eberheart can put off company work, so can I. When Cheryl arrived with the weekend mail, I pushed my work into a desk drawer. I told Cheryl I wasn't feeling well and I would be resting on the couch in the ladies' restroom. If someone came looking for me, I had an excuse for that one too. The sofa on the eighth floor was more comfortable. That was true but not good enough reason if anyone was digging around.

I milled around the eighth floor near the elevators looking for Janet. She came out heading for the bathroom. I followed her and did a repair job on my makeup. After she took care of business, she stepped up to the washbasins.

"I heard you have some problems with your computers," I said.

"How did you know?"

I introduced myself, told her where I worked and mentioned it would be this afternoon before anyone from C-T would have time to look at their computers.

She moaned. "The guys in my office are P. O.'d about the problem. If they have to wait very long they won't be fit to live with."

They'd be even more pissed off if they knew what Eberheart said about them. I asked her the questions CrackerJack fed me. She didn't know much but confirmed what was happening. I gave her the clues to solve the problem. "Just pass that on to your most experienced computer guy and you should be up and running in nothing flat."

She looked at me with a frown on her face.

"Look," I said, "I've learned a lot hanging around the guys in my office. Just don't tell anyone where you got the idea. If my boss at C-T finds out I screwed them out of billable hours, he'll flip his wig." I winked at Janet.

She returned the wink and left the restroom.

I no more than walked into C-T's offices when Cheryl answered the phone. "It's Boneventure," she said. "They don't need us—someone has already fixed their computers."

Heading for my cubicle, I smiled and did my best imitation of the Cheshire cat.

By eleven forty-five, my work was finished, and I went down to the lobby. I saw Janet Wilson in the middle of the atrium looking around. When she spotted me, she rushed over. "Can we have lunch together?"

"Of course," I said and wagged my head toward the food line. We settled into chairs at a small table, and she launched a speech, which sounded like it was well rehearsed. She told me she became the office hero with her knowledge of computers. She was embarrassed and wanted to give me credit. I pulled her up short and told her it was a lucky guess on my part. To myself I said, with a little help from CrackerJack. I also figured that gave me a great opportunity to pump her about the people in her office.

"I was wondering," I said, "did any of your people know the guys at Cyber-Technology very well?" She scrunched her mouth up and frowned like she was thinking, but didn't say a thing. "I mean, did they spend any time together or did they talk about them?"

That seemed to jog a mental synapse or two. I kept silent , and was ready to explode before she spoke.

"I almost hate to talk about him. 'Cause he's dead, you know."

I bit the inside of my lip. It was the only way I could keep my mouth shut. I was dying to ask her…What? Anything. Her mouth opened again and I was saved from blurting out something inane.

"Mr. Hawkins said he was talking to your office…a couple of weeks before he fell…before he died. I'm not sure what it was about, but he would really get, ah…agitated when he was on the phone to them."

I fiddled with the salt and pepper shakers on the table. Anything to keep me from saying something and breaking her train of thought. She was quiet again, so I shifted my attention to the little container holding white, blue and pink packets.

"I did hear Mr. Hawkins say one time when he was talking to someone named Ross—I guess that was Mr. Worthington—that he didn't think what was going on was kosher. I don't think Mr. Hawkins was Jewish. Was Mr. Worthington Jewish?"

I figured that one required an answer. "I don't know, but I don't think so. What else did they talk about?"

"I didn't hear much in the way of details, I just heard them talking about things. I know whenever Mr. Hawkins mentioned your company, Mr. Boneventure—my boss—Mr. Boneventure would nearly go ballistic. Usually they would go into my boss's office and slam the door. That's why I was such a hero this morning. We got our computer problem solved and didn't have to use Cyber-Technology. Are you sure I can't give you some credit for the solution?"

"Oh, please don't," I said hoping it sounded like humility. "After all, we don't want them to think anyone from Cyber-Technology came to their rescue." I winked. "Did Brian, I mean Mr. Hawkins, seem depressed or down the day he died?"

"No. As a matter of fact, that morning he was saying he and his family were going to take a long weekend. He was planning to leave Thursday morning—just two days after he died."

"Did the police talk to you when he fell?"

"Yes, but not for very long."

She smiled and looked at her watch. "I need to get back to work. Thanks again, Casey. If you ever need anything, give me a call. I owe you a big one."

22

THE NEXT MORNING, I WAS BUSY AT MY DESK WHEN
a shadow fell across the computer screen. I was surprised when I
looked up and saw Janet Wilson. She asked me if I was ready for
a break. I snatched my purse and led the way out of the office. I
didn't want people in my office associating me with Janet.

We each grabbed our favorite break repast—a latte and a
Danish—and settled into a pair of the more comfortable chairs
near the coffee bar. I gave her a couple of minutes to begin the
conversation.

"You know, Casey, yesterday you asked me if Mr. Hawkins
was depressed."

I nodded and thought, of course I do, sweetie. I was busy
pumping you for info.

"Well, last night I thought about him. You know, I told you
he was planning a long weekend for the coming Thursday. On
top of that he was proud of what he was doing with the company
and was looking forward to a promotion. He was in too good a
mood to even think about killing himself."

"Sometimes it's hard to tell. Some folks hide their feelings
pretty well," I said.

"Not him. Not that one. He wore his feelings and emotions
on his sleeve—out in the open." She leaned back in her chair and
cocked her head. "I also remembered some other conversations
about your company he had with my boss. Again, I only heard
bits and pieces. One time, it was 'fooling around with the files'
and another time it was something about 'could be costing us
money'—does that help you any?"

More than you can imagine, Janet, I thought. I was also beginning to wonder if she would ever ask the obvious.

As if she just read my mind, she said, "Why are you so interested in Mr. Hawkins?"

I came close to blowing a mouthful of coffee out my nose. I coughed and sputtered trying to think of a good answer. "Idle curiosity," was the best I could muster on short notice. She didn't press the issue, which gave me time to think. "I suppose since someone in my office died too, I'm looking around for connections. And, our two companies also did business together."

She nodded and said, "It does seem strange that two people in the same building commit suicide so close together."

The newer theory of the murder of Hawkins wasn't making the rounds of the offices. I'm sure if it was, Janet would have heard about it. I decided to press the issue with her. "Since you don't think Mr. Hawkins was the type to kill himself, what do you think happened?"

"I haven't thought about it." She looked up, down, side to side, all the time shaking her head. She turned her face back to me. "Was he killed?"

"Quite likely," I said. "Can you think of any reason someone would want him dead?"

Her eyes widened and she shook her head, so I tried another direction. "Could he have been fooling around? Could there be a jealous lover or a vengeful husband?"

"Oh, no. I don't think so. He was a devoted family man, always talking about his wife and children."

She kept coming back to the comments she heard about my company, but she couldn't put her finger on anything or anyone in particular. As if some lurking thought broke the surface, she took a quick intake of air and paused with her mouth open before she spoke.

"I remember…" Her eyes drifted. "I remember the day before…" Her eyes were moist. "I remember the day before Mr.

Hawkins died; he and Mr. Worthington met in the hallway out-side our office. I couldn't really hear what they were saying, but Mr. Hawkins was shaking his finger in Mr. Worthington's face like he was scolding him or warning him. Do you think Mr. Worthington could have killed Mr. Hawkins and then com-mitted suicide?"

"Anything's possible." I left the thought hanging in mid-air, but I didn't believe that scenario.

When I returned to the office, I saw Wayne Harmon and Winston Eberheart talking in the hallway. They saw me coming, grew silent and ducked into Wayne's office. I stopped around the corner from Wayne's door and listened. Their tones were hushed, but I heard enough. Eberheart went up to the Boneventure offices this morning to take a look at their computer trouble. He was told the problem was solved "in house" the previous day. Eberheart was ticked off at their attitude and said something like "I'll hit them harder the next time I dip into their client base." I thought that was a tacky attitude since only the day before he'd said he didn't care if they waited for help with their computer problems.

Just before lunch, I put in a call to CrackerJack. It took a while before he picked up. He spoke in a halting fashion and I could hear him pounding the keyboard in the background. He told me he was having trouble checking out the CT computer server. Something about size and space available not matching. "I'll have to do more work, Casey," he said. "And, I've got one more priority ahead of you. I should be able to get it done this afternoon, and I'll call you tonight. Okay?"

I agreed and hung up. There wasn't any way to rush him. After all, he was doing all the work gratis.

At noon, I was by the elevators in the lobby waiting for Janet Wilson to appear. She did and I pretended the meeting was a coincidence. We ate lunch, but she didn't have much to add to the morning's tidbits.

I spent the rest of the afternoon pretending to be busy at my desk. The pace of my workload was driving me crazy. I dug through more client emails on the server and transferred them to thumb drives, which now resided in my purse.

* * *

Later at home the same night, I told Aaron and Effie about the details I got from Janet Wilson. They were both as excited as I was. We could concentrate on motives rather than having to convince the police it was a murder. That left us with the dilemma of whether the second death was a murder…and the connection, if any.

"We should focus on the theory the two are connected," Effie said.

Aaron said, "Does that leave us with a murder and a remorseful suicide or two murders?"

"Two murders," was Effie's reply. "And, I think there is only one motive."

"How so?" Aaron said.

These two were on a roll, so I kept my mouth shut.

Effie twisted on the couch and tucked one leg under her. "We know there is some hanky-panky going on at Cyber-Technology. We know the accounting firm is a client and C-T is no doubt stealing from them in some fashion. Can't we assume Mr. Hawkins found out what C-T was doing and threatened to blow the whistle?"

Aaron stood up and started pacing. "So someone at Cyber-Technology kills Hawkins to stop him from exposing the fraud. Why is Ross Worthington killed? I don't think the murders are related, and that leaves us with another motive we haven't discovered."

Effie shook her head and said, "No." Aaron stared at her, but she stared back until he sat down. She went on, "If they are not related, then it's a coincidence that two people died in the same manner in such a short time. I don't believe in coincidences of that magnitude."

I found no valid argument against her theory and Aaron remained silent as well. The discussion went on for another two hours without further resolution. The phone interrupted us. It was CrackerJack calling as promised.

He told me the Cyber-Technology server intrigued him. By identifying the computer, he knew the amount of storage it should have. After measuring the used space and the free space, the numbers were about sixty percent of the total they should be. "Took me over an hour of steady keyboarding to break into the missing storage partition, Babe." CrackerJack gave me instructions on how to access the data and said, "Looks like it will be interesting reading. Your guys at C-T were not only stealing clients, but at least in one case, Ouachita Financial Planners, C-T was skimming money from their transactions—"

"How the heck did you uncover that?" I shouted at the speakerphone.

"Oh, didn't I ever tell you? My formal education was as a forensic accountant. It was fun for a while, but got too old, too quick. Computer consulting is a bunch more fun. Hey, that ain't all about Ouachita Financial…for the most part they are one big Ponzi scheme. They do have a legit segment of business, but they are ripping off a bunch of people. Another reason Cyber-Tech is getting gobs of money from them. It's all covered in that hidden section of their server."

"Wow, what do I do with that information?"

"Guess you better tell the cops when this thing winds up. Talk to you later, Casey."

As usual, the dial tone told me he didn't hang around for a response. I could picture him attacking his keyboard to solve his next mystery. Using the word attack, is not exaggerating. Some time ago, I learned his keyboards lasted a month or so. His constant banging puts them on the scrap heap way before their life expectancy runs out. He always keeps several spares handy.

I looked at the clock and decided it was too late to pursue

CrackerJack's lead. I recapped what he said with Effie and Aaron, and we settled in to watch the late-night news. PK wandered into the living room. Aaron went to the entryway closet and retrieved a small package from his jacket pocket. He unwrapped the plastic and dangled a toy mouse by its tail. PK's eyes locked onto the movement and he turned into a gray streak as Aaron let the mouse fly like a missile. "I thought a few toys might make PK stop attacking the walls," Aaron said.

"We'll see," I said. "I doubt it, but we'll see."

23

THE NEXT MORNING AT WORK, I CONTEMPLATED searching for the hidden server space on the Cyber-Technology computer CrackerJack told me about. It was an intriguing idea, but concern that someone from C-T might discover what I was doing made me decide to put it off. It would be far safer to try it from home when there was plenty of time to cover my tracks.

I decided to snoop around the paper files instead. Using the excuse of researching clients for my normal duties was decent cover. A trip to the file room allowed me to do a pretty good job of checking. I didn't find anything of interest pointing to the fraud we suspected. The only area left were the documents in Wayne Harmon's office. I didn't figure I could waltz in there and rummage through his files. That would take some privacy.

I managed to be around when Cheryl went to lunch. I suggested we walk to the River Market for something to eat. It was a bit warm, but the humidity was lower so the time outside was bearable. Between the walk there and back and the time over lunch, there was ample opportunity to pump Cheryl about Harmon's work habits. I used the running-behind-with-my-work ploy and I was thinking about coming back during the evening. I stressed two points: didn't want the boss to know my work was not getting done, and wouldn't be asking for extra pay for the overtime. "You know," I said, "I wouldn't want Mr. Harmon coming back into the office and finding me at my desk."

Cheryl was more than understanding and talked about her previous position where she could never get her work done during the day. "I know what you mean. I think you'll be safe. Mr. Harmon never works overtime. Especially at night."

When we returned to the office, she went to her desk and looked around to be sure no one was in sight. She withdrew a key and handed it to me. "This'll get you in C-T's front door," she whispered. "You'll have to get by the lobby guards on your own if you don't want Wayne, Mr. Harmon, to know you've been in the building."

I was able to reach Effie first and then Aaron by mid-afternoon. I wanted both to help me break into the files in Wayne's office. When I told them what we would be doing, the anticipation in their voices was evident.

The lure of seeing the "crime scene" on the tenth floor was an added incentive neither could resist. I gave Aaron a list of items to bring along and told them we would meet for dinner downtown around six. I asked Effie if she would have any problem getting into town. She said she was already busy with bus schedules and found the answer. Aaron balked at the idea of bringing my Glock along saying, "Casey, you may have a permit to carry a weapon, but I don't." I agreed with him and said we could do without it. Before leaving the ninth floor after work, I installed my name tag bar on the stairway door jamb in case we needed a secondary escape route.

∗ ∗ ∗

The three of us finished dinner by seven p.m. and headed for the Midtown Atrium Towers Building. Their voices seemed to be an octave higher than usual. I felt the same—the anticipation of breaking into the Cyber-Technology offices was revving my motor as well. Since I had a key to the C-T front door, I wondered if it was technically "breaking" into the place. Effie was the first to broach the subject of getting past the guards. I had mentioned guards earlier when I called them, but had no idea how we would accomplish this feat of derring-do.

Effie asked about the layout of the building lobby and where the guards and the stairs were located. I gave her a run-down on the geography and she was silent for several minutes. "All I need is the phone number for the security desk," she said. "I'll keep them busy on the phone while you and Aaron slip out of the door leading up from the parking garage into the building stairwell."

Aaron said, "You mean we have to walk up nine floors?"

"Yes," Effie said. "I bet the guards can see the elevator lights from where they sit, so we couldn't get to an upper floor without them noticing the elevators were being used."

I could still see a hole in the strategy. "How do you get past the guards, Effie?"

She looked around the street and ducked into a drug store. Effie displayed a bag of marbles when she emerged and said, "I'll roll a marble across the floor and when the guards seem distracted enough I'll follow you into the stairwell."

On the way to the cars, we stopped at a phone booth to consult a directory. It listed an after-hours phone number for the Midtown Atrium Towers Building and we figured it was a good number for the security desk.

24

EFFIE'S PLAN WORKED LIKE A CHARM—FOR THE MOST part. Coming up from the parking garage of the MAT building to the lobby, the stairwell side of the door was no problem—it had a crash bar. One thing I didn't remember in my run-down of the lobby layout was the large planter in front of the doors to the stairwells. It was almost in line with the guards' view of the doors we needed to use. It provided good cover for us as we exited the door from the parking garage and entered the one for the stairs going to the upper floors.

We arrived at the front door to Cyber-Technology, and the key Cheryl gave me got us in. Aaron stopped, leaned against the door jam panting and said, "Next time let's break into a two-story building."

Once inside, we made our way to Wayne's office. There were two file cabinets, both two-drawer models. A button with a key-hole above the top drawer on each told me they were locked. The buttons were pushed in and flush with the front. I punched and banged the buttons to no avail. Aaron stepped forward and reached into his hip pocket. He slid a couple of slim metal tools into the lock on one cabinet. He jiggled and twisted them and the lock popped out. He slid a drawer open and went to work on the second file.

We found enough incriminating evidence on C-T to do a Clint Eastwood version of "Hang 'Em High." As I worked my way through the files, Effie made copies of thirty to forty documents. When I thought we had enough confirmation of the facts, we made sure all the original paperwork was back in the proper folders and locked both cabinets.

I tucked the stack of documents into the back of my belt, under my shirt and said, "How 'bout a trip to the tenth floor?"

My name badge magnet was still in place to allow us to reenter the ninth floor if necessary. Aaron and Effie were impressed with the trick, and I realized I hadn't shared that one with them.

I led the way to the twelfth floor and down the two "ladders" to ten. The emergency lighting on these floors, even under construction, was enough to make our way. We used our flashlights to probe the darker recesses. We were careful not to allow the beams of light to be visible to the lobby guards.

As I expected, we didn't find anything. We retraced our steps back up the ladders and down the stairwell to the ninth floor. I retrieved my name badge backing and we descended to the lobby. Slipping from one doorway to the other was a bit trickier than before. Effie went first and crouched behind the planter. She waved us through as one of the guards stood up and turned toward us. Aaron and I ducked out of sight before the guard turned far enough to face us, but he must have seen the door swing shut. He shouted our direction, "Who the hell is over there?" He turned back to his partner and Effie sailed a couple of marbles toward the other side of the atrium. "What the hell was that?" the second guard said. They both turned to face the sound and Effie waved us through the door to the garage. I heard more marbles bouncing across the tile floor and Effie followed us into the stairwell.

On the way out of the garage, I realized that using Ross Worthington's key card to enter was registered on the MAT security system. As we drove back to Aaron's car I put in a call to CrackerJack. I explained the problem and he said he could log onto the MAT server and erase any trace we left behind entering the parking garage. "Now you're learning to think like a real cracker, Casey," he said.

At home, the three of us sat down at the kitchen table to compare notes about the evening's excursion. Effie may have expressed it best when she told us her heart was still thumping and she'd never in her life done anything as exciting.

I agreed with her, but I wasn't about to let the others know. Us gals got some of those macho genes too.

Aaron was anxious to compare some of the copied paperwork from the Cyber-Technology files with the information we pulled from the emails and the server hacking. Effie wanted to talk about getting into and out of the building lobby. "Did you see how well those marbles bouncing across the tile floor distracted the guards?" she said.

She was proud of her part in the escapade and I agreed with her again. This time I spoke up and complimented her resourcefulness. Aaron was also generous with his praise.

We spent a few more minutes covering the actual evidence we found. No specific conclusions came to our minds, so we decided to pack it in for the night. We would have time the next night to go deeper into the details.

Early the following morning, I asked Effie if she could snoop into the bank records of Ouachita Financial Planners and the Austin Consultants. I was looking for large transactions indicating big deals coming their way. I wanted to compare the dates of those transactions with the dates where C-T conducted visits to their clients' servers.

Effie told me she would have to do it today. She planned on leaving early tomorrow afternoon for a weekend visit to her family. "I worked it out with my boss," she said. "He said I could leave around three so I could catch my bus back home."

"Do what you can today, then. Anything will help. When are you planning to return to Little Rock?"

"My bus gets back mid-afternoon on Sunday. You'll have the weekend to yourself, Casey."

"Oh, well. We can do more computer snooping next week," I said.

I was wondering about Aaron when she added, "Aaron told me he leaves tomorrow morning and will be gone until Monday evening."

I contemplated an entire weekend on my own. Well, not quite on my own. A vision of Dennis, sans towel, popped into my head.

25

FRIDAYS ARE ALWAYS LIGHT AT CYBER-TECHNOLOGY. I decided to get my normal duties out of the way so I could devote the rest of the day to whatever snooping might be in order.

Janet Wilson from Boneventure was in the lobby when I went for my morning break. She thanked me again for making her the office hero for their computer problem earlier in the week. I was emphatic that she not give me any credit. She kept saying I deserved it, and it was tough playing humble—covering the fact I didn't want anyone to know I was digging around.

The subject changed back to the employees of the companies we worked for. "I've been wondering if someone other than Wayne Harmon actually runs our office," I said.

"It's funny you say that. I've heard some of our people refer to Mr. Eberheart more often than Mr. Harmon. When I finally heard Harmon's name, I asked who he was."

Suspicions confirmed, I thought. That backed up what Cheryl told me. "Have you heard anything else that seemed out of place?" I asked.

"You remember I told you about Mr. Hawkins waving his finger at Mr. Worthington?" I nodded and she continued, "Well…I almost hate to say this…"

She seemed to be winding down and I was afraid she would drop the thought. "Janet, you know I would never repeat anything you tell me. You know you can trust me, don't you?"

She sat there, not moving, for a minute or two. Then she said, "I heard more than one person say Mr. Hawkins better be careful…"

Another long silence, so I said, "Careful?…About what?"

"I'm not sure, but they seemed to be afraid of Mr. Eberheart—like he might do something to them…"

"Like what? To the business or to them personally?"

Janet looked into my eyes and I got the impression there was fear behind the words she spoke. "I think they were afraid for themselves, not the business."

"Are you telling me they were more afraid of Mr. Eberheart than they were of Mr. Harmon?"

Janet nodded her head and by now I figured we'd exhausted the subject, so we switched to men. I told her of my plans to invite a friend to my place for dinner tomorrow night. "You got any ideas for a meal?"

"Is it light conversation or a candlelight setting that could lead to heavy breathing?"

I was blushing. I could feel the crimson creeping up my face. "I'm not sure, but I'm hoping for the latter." Now, I could tell the flush was showing.

We discussed a few strategies and meals. It was unfortunate her idea of cooking exceeded my culinary skills. I thanked her for the ideas and we both headed back to work.

I breezed through the glass doors to the Cyber-Technology office and Cheryl handed me a pink phone message slip. "He called a couple of minutes ago," she said.

The "From" line read: Dennis. I rushed to my cubicle and dialed the number. When I identified myself, he said, "That was quick." He told me he was on his way out of the building and was wondering if he could stop by my office.

I said, "Yes, I'd love to see you." I'm going to scare him off if I'm not careful I told myself. We confirmed a time and hung up. I leaned back, basking in the warm glow flowing through my body. "Better to deliver an invitation in person than over the phone." I looked around to be sure nobody heard my comment. I spent the next several minutes rehearsing the dinner invitation.

* * *

By the time I got home, everyone else was gone. There was a note from both Aaron and Effie confirming they were on their way. Aaron was on a three-day trip and would not return until Monday, and Effie confirmed her bus would not arrive back in Little Rock until late on Sunday afternoon.

I grabbed the two cookbooks I own, a pad of paper and a pencil. I had no idea in the world what I could prepare that would put Dennis in the mood…but at least there were twenty-four hours to figure it out.

26

SATURDAY DISPLAYED THE FACE OF A BRIGHT AND happy child, but it didn't help as I wrestled with the menu problem. Friday night I was enjoying a warm glow, but I still have no meal ideas this morning. Facing such a fine day, I knew I could solve the tightest Gordian knot. Problem is, I didn't know any Girl Scouts with a merit badge in knots—nor did I know how I could prepare an intimate dinner.

Where is Effie when I need her? She would have been able to whip up a seven-course masterpiece and hand me the warming instructions as she walked out the door. Somehow, I would have to solve that one on my own.

Several sheets from a yellow pad were already crumpled and lying on the floor when I experienced an epiphany. Among the many courses I took as Jarvis the Rat's wife was one from the chef of a four-star restaurant in the Heights. I called, pulled her away from her luncheon crowd and explained my predicament. She laid out the menu, told me her sous chef would do most of the work. In a couple of cases, the meal would be prepared and all I needed to do was heat it at the appropriate time. Others would come in "pieces" which even I could assemble into a tasty course.

She laid the final details on me—the cost. "This meal will run around one hundred and twenty-five dollars—per person." She was polite enough to give me a minute to recover both my composure and breath and added, "And if I didn't owe you a big one, you'd have to take out a loan for it. As it is, I'll charge you for the fixin's. How does fifty bucks sound?"

I did a big gulp and leaped at the proposal. She even offered to have one of her staff deliver everything, including dishes and serving pieces.

* * *

Dennis arrived and the preliminaries went well. A glass of White Zinfandel gave us both a glow. I followed my chef friend's notes and the meal was an enormous success. I even amazed myself. Dennis was lavish with his praise and offered to help me with the dishes. It was the first time I could remember I enjoyed washing dishes.

We retired to the living room with a final drink—a snifter of Courvoisier. The glow was growing brighter—there was a glowing fire in the fireplace and I don't have a fireplace. The television would have to do. I surfed the channels looking for the most romantic movie I could find, not wanting Dennis to get interested in some macho action flick.

He and I were sitting close to one another on the couch. I kicked off my shoes, curled my legs under me and leaned closer to Dennis. He slipped his shoes off, propped his feet on the coffee table and put his arm along the back of the sofa. My love life was looking up.

His arm slid down from the back of the couch and rested on my shoulders. I leaned against him and nestled as close as possible. We both lost interest in the movie and I tilted my face up to his lips. He took the hint and we began a session of open-mouth tongue wrestling I found pleasurable. I was getting hotter and I felt his hand working on the buttons of my blouse. I leaned back and made a sound I hoped was one of encouragement. Three buttons later his hand rested on my breast and I was squirming closer.

I opened my mouth to suggest we move to my bedroom when I heard a noise at the front door. I looked up to see Aaron coming in with his overnight bag. It was obvious from the look on his face he wasn't expecting to find anyone in the living room—let alone his landlady and a policeman in the initial stages of undress.

"Hi, Dennis," he said. He nodded and wagged his head toward me and was unable to find any words. With an "oops" expression on his face he ducked into his room and emerged a minute later with a shaving kit in his hand. "I've got a sleep-over. See you all later."

He was out the door in thirty seconds. I looked at Dennis and he looked at me. We both straightened our bodies and our clothes and went back to watching TV. I didn't bother to button my blouse. It took a good fifteen minutes, but by then we were back into the wrestling position that Aaron interrupted. I could feel Dennis leaning toward me so I let him guide me into a more supine position. He was moving his leg and I knew it would be over mine in a minute. I spread mine. His thigh pressed down on me between my legs. I arched my back and met his pressure as he unbuttoned the rest of my blouse. Reaching down, I inched my skirt up toward my hips, and began to work on his belt.

I was hot. Dennis was hot—I think it was obvious to both of us. There was more than his thigh pressing against me. I said, "Dennis, wouldn't we be more comfortable—"

The front door to my condo opened again and Effie whisked into the living room. She stopped about fifteen feet in front of us. "Hi, Casey," she said. Then turning her attention to Dennis, said, "I'm Effie Tremayne."

Dennis scrambled to a semi-upright position and introduced himself. Effie was oblivious to the sweaty passion confronting her. She sat down and explained her visit to her family didn't go well. During the third argument, she tossed her belongings into her bag and headed back to the bus depot. She finally became aware of my sideways head nods and eye rolls. Looking at me, then at Dennis, she said, "I guess I'll get to bed now."

Dennis and I watched a few more minutes of the movie. I was explaining to him that Effie was a super sound sleeper and we could still retire to my bedroom.

"I'm sorry, Casey," he said. I could feel the evening and the rest of the night slipping away. He wasn't able to look at me when he said, "Maybe we could pick up again some other night."

Nothing between my legs tonight, I thought. "Next time, I'll change the lock on the front door." My attempt to lighten the atmosphere was not perceptible on his face. The goodnight kiss was long and passionate, so there were hopes for the future. Now all that was left to do was strangle Effie and Aaron.

I went to my bathroom to get ready for bed. During the process of removing makeup I used a liberal amount of cold water on my face to reduce the earlier glow. It wasn't working well; I could still feel his leg between mine. I left my panties on, pulled on an old T-shirt I use for a nightgown and threw my robe around my shoulders.

I made my last round of the condo, checking lights and security. I was about to leave the living room for my room when I heard a light tapping at the front door. Dennis decided to come back. Racing to the door, I forgot a cardinal security rule—always check the peephole. I yanked the door open and said, "Dennis…"

27

I WAS FACING A TALL MAN WEARING ALL BLACK including the ski mask. Before I could take a breath, he pushed me back and dragged me inside. "Where's your bedroom?" he said.

I started to yell, but the man in black whacked me across the face. I could feel the sting and my skin turning red. I said, "What do you want? I have a little money here. You can have it." I was trying to slow him down.

"Which way?" I nodded the proper direction. He spun me, wrapped his arms around me from behind and lifted. We were moving toward my bedroom with my feet dangling an inch or so off the floor. I struggled as hard as possible, but he had me on weight, height and upper body strength. I twisted and did my best to remember my self-defense training.

"Anyone else here?" he demanded.

This time I paid attention to his voice. It was deep, husky and seemed forced. Disguising it, I thought.

"Well?"

"No," I said. "I'm the only one here." Effie's room was on the other side of the condo and with luck I could get rid of the creep before he found her.

"I think that's bullshit, Lady. I know the black bastard's gone. Where's the other bitch?"

I hoped my surprise didn't show. He seemed to know a lot about me and my roommates. "You must be mistaken. I am the only one here."

He kept dragging me toward my room. We reached the foot of the bed with my feet still dangling. I was waiting for him to put me down, so I could make a move to escape. I wasn't fast enough. He lowered me and gave me a vicious push toward the bed. As I was propelled forward, he stripped the bathrobe off my shoulders. I bounced on the bed and he leapt onto the bed next to me. I tried to roll off the side, but he grabbed my arm and flipped me on my back. Before I could move, he was kneeling between my legs, forcing them apart with his knees and pinning my arms down over my head.

I concentrated on his appearance. He was dressed in black from head to toe. A bit of his face showed behind the mask. He was white. Sleeves down to his wrists and leather gloves—no identifying marks visible. I estimated him at about five foot eleven and a hundred and seventy to eighty pounds. His weight pressing down on me felt heavier. Unless I could get the mask off, there was no way I could ever identify him. I tested the resistance of his grip, and every time I moved an arm or hand, he squeezed harder.

He rose up, let one of my arms go and hooked the fingers of one hand into my panties. He tore at them, but the elastic was too tough to give. He reached into a pocket and pulled out a knife. He pressed a button and the switch blade snicked open. He made two quick slices and my panties were no longer an obstacle. He released my other arm and said, "If you move or try to get away, I'll smack you so hard the ringing in your head will never stop."

I laid still and judged my chances. He reached for his crotch and pulled his penis out of his pants. He was already wearing a condom. Son-of-a-bitch, I thought. He won't even leave DNA behind. I clawed at him hoping for a bit of skin under a nail, but all I felt was leather and cloth. I tried to squirm away. He stopped me and put one hand on my chest. The other hand was on my throat and he began squeezing. "Relax and enjoy it, bitch," he said.

He continued squeezing my throat and I could feel my consciousness slipping away. The room was getting dimmer. I knew there were but a few seconds left to do something or I might be unconscious or dead when he raped me. My arms flailed out, grasping and grabbing and finding nothing. Then my left hand banged the nightstand and I clawed at it. My hand found the Trimline phone and my fingers curled around it. With my last ounce of energy I swung the instrument at a spot I judged to be his head.

He grunted as the phone smashed into his temple and the bell tinkled. He sagged forward and I put both hands up and pushed him to the side where he collapsed on the bed. My head was beginning to clear. I rolled the bastard over on his back and jumped between his legs. He was groaning and moving his head like he was headed back to the world of the living. I needed to send him back out there. I knelt between his legs with my hands on his chest. I said, "Relax and enjoy it… " I extended my right leg straight out behind me. "Asshole." The word exploded from my mouth as I brought my right knee down and forward with as much power as I could marshal. It collided with his groin with enough force to pop the rubber off. I guess when the testicles are mashed, the penis tends to shrink. He was groaning but motionless.

Sliding down toward the foot of the bed, I tied the laces of his black sneakers together. I moved around the side of the bed and tugged the ski mask off and tossed it away. I got a good look at his face but didn't recognize him. I grabbed for the phone cord figuring it would be good for tying his hands.

I reached for his wrists and he swung an arm at me. It caught me off guard, sending me reeling backward. He rolled off the bed and started to run. The shoelace trick did the job. He crashed to the floor in a heap of confusion. I rummaged in my panty drawer and located the Glock. The loaded magazine was one drawer down and I was going for it.

He looked down wondering why his feet weren't working. Seeing the tied laces he kicked the sneaks off and jumped to his feet. I didn't figure I had the strength to stop him, so I concentrated on slamming the magazine into the butt of the automatic and pulling the slide back to put a round into the chamber.

He saw what I was doing, snatched up his mask and sneakers and raced for the front door. I watched the retreating figure, looking for anything more to help identify him. There wasn't much to see. I couldn't shoot him in the back—my stupid training kicked in again. Even inside my home, it's tough to explain shooting someone in the back. But, if he turns around I'll put three in his chest, I told myself.

I followed him into the living room. He slammed the front door shut behind him. I sat down and put the gun next to me on the couch. Next I grabbed my phone and dialed Dennis. When he answered, I could tell he was still in his car heading home. I told him what happened with as much calm as I could collect. I was beginning to experience post-trauma adrenaline let down. My voice was quivering and I think it upset Dennis. I assured him I was okay, but he didn't sound satisfied.

"Casey, I want you to hang up and call 9-1-1. Tell them what happened, give as good a description as you can, stay on the phone until they arrive and tell them there is a plain-clothes cop responding to the scene."

I could hear the sound of a siren and tires squealing before he punched the END button on his cell phone.

28

THERE WAS A KNOCK ON THE DOOR AND SOMEONE shouted "police." I picked up the gun and told them the door was unlocked. Two uniformed officers eased into the room. They spotted my weapon and their right hands went to their holsters.

"Put the gun down, Ma'am."

The voice was loud, but not a shout. It was also firm and implied failure to comply would bring retaliation. I did what he said. I looked down at myself and realized I was still in my T-shirt and no panties. I was about to suggest I get a robe when Dennis appeared at the doorway. His hand was extended over his head, his badge visible and he said, "I'm on the job."

The second officer verified his ID and they all approached me. "Dennis," I said, "would you get me a robe. There's one at the foot of my bed." I pointed toward my room.

Dennis draped the robe over my shoulders and sat down next to me. I told them the entire story: from my failure to check the peephole to the policemen entering the condo. Dennis and the police officer with notepad in hand, asked several questions.

I'd covered all the details and had nothing more to add. A shiver shook my entire body as I thought about the events and what might have happened. The cop said, "So, you were alone here in the residence?"

I did a total double-take. The fact Effie was in her bedroom, apparently still asleep, had escaped me. "No. There's another woman here," I said pointing toward her room.

Dennis stood up and started for her door. "Don't startle her," I said. "She's a sound sleeper."

"I guess she is," he said.

Dennis got Effie settled down next to me and went to the kitchen while I recounted the details of the last hour to her.

Effie looked at me and said, "Why didn't you yell at me? Why didn't you yell for help?"

"I hoped that no matter what happened, he wouldn't know you were here."

The police went back to their questions. "Then there's nothing he left behind. Nothing that might carry his DNA?" I was silent and he continued, "You didn't scratch him?" I was still silent. "Do you think the phone you used to hit him might have some blood or skin on it?"

"I suppose it could. You're more than welcome to take it for testing." Something in the back of my head was swirling around trying to get out. What was it? "Wait…the condom." I realized I'd forgotten a major detail. "I didn't tell you about the condom. It popped off when I kneed him. I don't think he picked it up. If he didn't, then it's still somewhere in the bed clothes." I started to get up. "Should I go look for it?" The cop taking notes shook his head and I sat down again.

Dennis returned with two cups of steaming coffee. He went back to the kitchen to retrieve one for himself. "I called the Crime Scene Unit folks while I was in the kitchen. They'll be here in a half hour."

Dennis pulled out a notepad and looked at me. "Let's get to the 'why' of what happened. Casey, do you think this was a random attack?"

"What else could it be?" I could see Dennis was waiting for a better answer. "You don't think it could be related to what's going on at the Midtown Atrium Towers Building, do you?"

"I think maybe it could," he said. "If someone there learned you are snooping around, they may have decided to stop you."

29

DENNIS SPENT THE NIGHT ON THE COUCH. I TOLD him he could use Aaron's bedroom, but he said he preferred to be between the front door and the rest of us. We got to bed around three a. m. and none of us awoke until mid-morning.

We were gathering in the kitchen, deciding on a brunch menu. Effie was breaking eggs and talking about omelets. Dennis and I deferred to her suggestions. The front door opened. Dennis snatched his holster from the counter nearby and removed the service weapon, then stepped into the living room with the two of us close behind.

Aaron stopped in mid-stride and put both hands up in front of him—palms out and said, "Whoa."

Dennis slid the automatic back into its holster and Aaron moved toward us.

"Dennis was here all night," Effie said.

Aaron nodded. "I know."

"You know about the attack and that Dennis stayed here to protect us?"

"No. I knew Dennis was here last night and I figured he would stay...Ah...what attack?"

Effie took charge and told him what I related to her about the intruder. She stopped talking in mid-breath and said to Aaron, "How did you know Dennis was here?"

He explained how he walked in on Dennis and me and then left again.

She then recounted the part she witnessed after Dennis got her up. That didn't take long. Another mid-breath pause, and then she said, "Are omelets okay with you for breakfast?" He nodded and she disappeared into the kitchen.

After the dishes were cleared from the table, we all poured a cup of fresh coffee. The four of us went over the details of the deaths of Hawkins and Worthington. My roommates and I reaffirmed our belief the fraud Cyber-Technology was involved in, was somehow tied to those murders.

Dennis was still reluctant to accept our theories without more concrete evidence. I switched tracks. "Then tell us about the evidence collected on the tenth floor and the lobby. Maybe it'll ring a bell for someone."

Dennis covered as much as he could from memory—from the indications of disturbed dust up on ten to the blood swabs taken in the lobby. "That's pretty much it," he said, "except for the personal effects of the victims."

It seemed like he was winding down. I said, "So give. What's in those evidence bags?"

"Mostly the usual stuff—wallets, combs, handkerchiefs, coins and keys. 'Bout the only differences were a pocket knife Worthington was carrying and a beaded chain Hawkins had."

I shook my head. "What do you mean—beaded chain?"

"You know. A chain made up of little beads—like you use to hold keys together or those pull chains on overhead fans and lamps."

I think the three of us got the idea and Dennis added, "Must have fallen out of a pocket. It was under his body in the lobby."

"Any idea what it was for?" I asked.

Dennis frowned and said, "Nope. No idea. It didn't have one of those connector things on it. You know, the piece that locks the two ends together."

The four of us fell silent. I was letting my mind plow through what Dennis told us, turning the evidence over for a fresh view, doing my best to make sense of it. I was looking for a new connection. I sensed a light going on, but as I looked around, the whatever-it-was, flickered out.

Dennis arranged for a forensic artist to interview me at police headquarters.

* * *

Rachel Culpepper invited me to sit next to the desk holding her computer and a large sketchpad. She talked to me about the details of the attack and how I was able to escape and see the intruder's face.

"Bet you're wondering if I'm ever going to get to work on a picture," she said.

"I suppose you look at the whole scene before you start a sketch."

"You got it. Now, let's go for the face you remember."

Rachel talked, asked questions, sketched on the pad and manipulated a computer program. When I tried to sneak a peek at her work, she held up a finger. "In a minute. I like to get your general impressions down first. Then I'll have you check the drawing and the computer screen for corrections."

Thirty minutes into the session she motioned me to slide my chair around the desk. The chair rollers bumped over cracks in the tile floor. I could see her drawing and the computer monitor. I was amazed. Both images were good likenesses of my attacker.

Rachel said, "Now let's put in the details that'll round him out."

For another fifteen minutes we adjusted a jaw line, the mouth and eyebrows. "Wait a minute," I said. "His hair's parted on the wrong side. I told you right side, but that was looking at him. From his side, it would be the left."

Rachel smiled. "That was going to be my next question. Good catch. How about the teardrop tattoo by his eye?"

I closed my eyes and brought an image into focus. "That was on his right cheek."

A couple of mouse clicks and the hair part and tattoo moved to their proper locations.

"That's him," I said.

"Casey, I want you to close your eyes and visualize your bedroom Saturday night. Go through the attack and his escape in as much detail as you can. If it gets too uncomfortable, stop. Keep your eyes closed until I tell you to open them." She looked at me and said, "Ready? Close your eyes."

I did as she instructed and reached the point where I was sitting on the couch waiting for the police to arrive.

"Open your eyes, Casey," Rachel said.

The image on the computer screen leaped out at me and I gasped, "That is him."

Dennis said, "You done good, gal."

Rachel added, "You may be the best subject I've worked with."

Dennis pulled three copies of the computer image from a nearby printer and we headed for the parking lot. On the way home, I asked him for one of the pictures.

"What for?" he said.

I winked. "For the building grapevine."

"If this gets out, I'm in deep doo-doo. Be careful with my career…and be damn careful around the grapevine."

30

LOOKING BACK OVER THE WEEKEND'S EVENTS, EVEN the dark clouds and rain couldn't dampen my spirits this morning. I left home early, so I could drop Effie at her workplace and take surface streets downtown. Monday morning rush was moving slower than usual due to the slick streets. I smiled to myself. The attack could have been a lot worse—a whole lot worse. The windshield wipers were going swoosh…swoosh, brushing away a light mist. At a red light, I was humming along with the radio. I burst into song waving my arms to the music—directing the orchestra. I glanced to my right at the car stopped next to me. The gentleman displayed an expression on his face that said—if she gets out of her car, I'm driving up on the sidewalk to get away.

I stopped singing and waving, and stared at him for several seconds, then gave him a big stage wink. Looking straight ahead, he punched the accelerator hard when the light turned green.

I cut south to Markham Street and passed police headquarters. I waved at Dennis. He wasn't anywhere in sight, but I waved and blew him a kiss anyway.

I'll call him from work and invite him to dinner next weekend. That time I could rent motel rooms for Aaron and Effie and double-bolt the front door. If I kept the Glock loaded and handy, I could shoot anyone who tried to interrupt us. "Big talk, Casey. You'll probably wuss out and never get him into bed."

Just before my morning break, Aaron called. He told me he saw the note I left earlier and could meet me for lunch. We set the details and planned our meeting for the Midtown Atrium Towers Building lobby.

Eberheart was out of the office today on a client consultation. A couple of weeks back, I stopped by his office and attempted to engage him in conversation. His side of it was more like a series of grunts. I asked whether the door inside his office was another storage room. His response was, "If I thought a damned temp worker needed to know, I'd have told you."

So much for small talk. Since then, I've tried to open the door several times—when Eberheart was out of the office, of course. It was always locked.

I slipped into his office and tried the door again. Still locked. I made a note of the lock name and type.

I also snooped through Cyber-Technology's computer files looking for dates—dates of C-T visits to Boneventure Accounting and the Ouachita Financial Planners—and contacts with companies who were potential competitors of those clients. I also listed major deposits on both sides of those dates.

* * *

Aaron was already seated in the cafe when I arrived in the lobby. The stack of folders I asked him to bring were on the table.

We found matching dates and money. C-T's records showed Ouachita's bid for a big contract with a large legal firm. One day after that, another company, Jackson Financial Planning, PA, got the contract. Several days later, a substantial deposit from Jackson showed up in C-T's bank account. When I was searching the areas CrackerJack told me about and found traces of the Ponzi scheme Ouachita was running. I also located the places where C-T was electronically skimming a bit off each transaction Ouachita was involved in.

We uncovered a similar situation with Boneventure Accounting. It looked like Cyber-Technology tipped off a company named

Weston & Weston. Again, W & W underbid Boneventure and a large "retainer" appeared on C-T's books from them.

"Based on the legal courses I've taken," I said, "this would be categorized as circumstantial evidence. But…if they follow the money far enough, it could turn into hard evidence."

"Do you think there's a smoking gun in there somewhere?" Aaron said.

"It could also be a motive for murder. If Hawkins at Boneventure got wind of this, it might be the reason someone helped him off the tenth floor balcony."

"What's next?"

"Are you available Friday afternoon?"

Aaron told me he was scheduled for an out-and-back on Wednesday, but beyond that he wasn't on the flight schedule for over a week. I showed him my note about the door lock in Eberheart's office. "Could you pick a lock like that?"

"Should be a breeze. When and where?"

I told him about the door and my plans. "Be here about four on Friday. I can get everything set, and I'll tell you all about it at home tonight."

31

TUESDAY AND WEDNESDAY FLEW BY. I DROPPED
several comments and hints to Cheryl. I learned everyone in
the office planned to leave by noon on Friday to get a jump on
the Labor Day weekend. Everyone except Cheryl, that is. She
wanted to get away, but was stuck with closing the office at half
past five. By Thursday, I was ready to close the deal.

"Cheryl, I don't have anywhere to go this weekend. Afraid
I'm an old stick-in-the-mud." I let the idea sink in during lunch.

I could see the wheels turning in her head. "Do you still have
the office key I loaned you?" she said.

She was rising to the bait—time to set the hook. "Do you
need it back?"

"No. As a matter of fact I was going to ask you a favor."

On the off chance she was thinking of something else, I said,
"Do you want me to cover for you tomorrow afternoon?" Reel
in slow and steady, I thought.

She nodded.

Reach for the net; she's almost in the boat.

"The boss'll be mad if he finds out," Cheryl said.

I wondered which boss she meant—Harmon or Eberheart.
"No one will find out from me." I reached across the table and
patted her arm. "The bosses will be gone by noon and you can
be on the road by one."

* * *

That evening at home, we talked about the door in Eberheart's
office. I also showed the image of my attacker to Effie.

Effie was disappointed she would be left out of the upcoming caper. Due to my anticipated assignation with Dennis this weekend, she was planning another family visit.

"This is another branch of the family," she said. "We don't fight and I'll be able to stay all the way through Monday."

Earlier, Aaron also assured me he'd be gone by noon on Saturday and promised no surprise returns. He said, "How about tomorrow afternoon?"

"Be there by four-thirty and we'll find out what's behind mystery door number one," I said.

* * *

Molasses at the North Pole moves faster than the clock in my cubicle. The fact I was checking it every three minutes didn't help. There was nothing anywhere in or on my desk, which held my attention more than a few minutes. A morning break and lunch with Cheryl was no distraction. She gushed thanks for giving her an opportunity for an early start on the weekend and went on and on about her current boyfriend. She talked about her plans with him over the next three nights.

I thought if I paid attention, I could get some pointers on seducing the male of my choice. Cheryl crowed about the Bed and Breakfast where they would be staying. She went over the wardrobe she packed and described in detail the underwear in her suitcase—push-up, demi bras, thongs, hose and garter belts topped the list. Most of it was black and red she told me. For the more demure moments, she also included see-through waltz length peignoirs—again in red and black.

My mind drifted. I didn't have a single item in my chest of drawers similar to what she described. For a moment, I wondered if there was time for a quick trip to Victoria's Secret. Even if there was time, I thought, I wouldn't have the guts to wear them.

* * *

Both hands on the clock pointed straight up. The offices emptied. By twelve-thirty, Cheryl was getting jumpy and announced her departure.

"Fine," I said. Four hours until Aaron arrives. I'll be a raving looney by then, I told myself.

At quarter past four, the phone rang. I assured Aaron the coast was clear and met him at C-T's front door a few minutes later. I waved him around the corner, out of sight, and locked the entry door. Leading him to Eberheart's office, I pointed to the door. He made quick work of the lock.

"Wait a minute," I said. "I'm going to put my name tag magnet on the stairwell door on this floor. Just in case we need a second escape route."

I was back in Eberheart's office in under three minutes. Aaron twisted the knob and eased the door open. There wasn't much on the other side—a small concrete platform with a railing and dozens of large tubes running up and down the walls.

"I think it's a utility core," he said.

"What's it for?"

"The builders can run all the utilities, gas, electric, water, whatever they need, up a single shaft and branch out from here to each floor." Aaron stepped through the doorway and examined the other side. "You need a key to access this from your side, but from out here there is a thumb release to open it."

He tested the release to be sure. I moved through and saw a vertical ladder of sorts. The rungs were inch thick U's set into the concrete walls and they were surrounded by a steel cage. I suppose the cage was designed to keep one from falling, but it looked more like something a body would bump against all the way to the bottom.

"Let's go for the tenth floor," Aaron said.

He was right. There was a similar platform and door on the next floor up, which opened at his touch.

Aaron was whispering. "If Eberheart killed Hawkins, this explains how he did it and got away. That's assuming he has a key to the doors."

We moved inside. Since the floor was familiar to both of us, we didn't venture far from our escape door. Aaron clamped a hand on my wrist and put his other hand to my mouth. When he saw I was going to remain silent, the hand on my mouth slid away and he pointed to our left. I saw it. The beam of a flashlight played around near the spot where the bodies went over the railing and fell to their deaths.

With his mouth to my ear, he said, "Who the hell would be up here?"

His voice was so low I strained to hear him. I shook my head and shrugged. "Flashlight" was moving through the shadows and I couldn't make out any features. From the size, I figured it was a man. He edged into some light coming from the atrium area. It was my turn to grab Aaron's arm. "Damn. It's Eberheart." The adrenaline was pumping and my heart began to race.

I felt the panic rise in my throat. I swallowed hard and fought it back while we moved toward our get-away route. I kicked a piece of metal and it sounded like thunder in the quiet.

"Who the hell is back there?" It was Eberheart's voice.

"We need to get out of here," I said.

Aaron pulled the door open and pushed me through. "Get started back down to nine. I'll do some escape and evasion to throw him off the scent."

I followed his instructions. He was still peering through the partly open door when I disappeared through the doorway into Eberheart's office. I said a silent prayer for Aaron and wondered what was on his mind. I looked down and noticed I'd tracked some whitish dust onto the carpet. I scuffed my shoes across it until it blended in and disappeared.

* * *

I hid in the corridor inside Cyber-Technology and peeked through the foliage of a ficus tree to keep an eye on the front door. Eberheart appeared, approached the door and rattled it. Getting no answer, he banged a fist on the glass. I wonder why he just doesn't unlock it and come in, I asked myself. Lazy? He turned, stalked off to the elevators and was gone.

I maintained my vantage point and waited. After an eternity passed, Aaron came into sight, keeping a sharp watch over his shoulder.

I let him in and shoved him down the hall toward the break room. "What happened? How the hell did you give him the slip?"

"If you'll stop asking questions, I'll tell you…I saw he was heading toward me, so I waited until he was close and slammed the door. He would have to dig out a key, if he had one, to follow me. With that head start, I was at the door on the eighth floor by the time he was on the ladder." He paused to see if I was still involved in his tale. I was, so he continued, "The rest was easy. On eight, I got an elevator, reached in and punched the button for four and let the door close without me. I hit the stairs and came up to this floor. As they say, the rest is history."

"Did you know he came here to the C-T door?"

"Yes. I was hiding in the stairwell. He must have tried to track me down to the fourth floor. He was gone long enough. After he left here, I gave him time to leave before you saw me in the hall."

I didn't have much to add and could think of no more questions, except "Did he see you?"

"Not up close, but he probably knows I'm black."

"It's time to close up shop for the day," I said.

Aaron said, "Come on old Paint, let's get where we ain't, said Tonto to his faithful steed, Scout."

I did a double-take eye roll and said, "Sounds like a good idea, but we'd better not leave together. Eberheart could be in the lobby looking for you."

32

AT MY CONDO, AARON AND I COMPARED NOTES. Neither of us saw Eberheart on our way out of the Midtown Atrium Towers Building, nor did we notice any vehicles following us on the way home.

I used my cell phone coming out I-630 to order Chinese take-out. The delivery guy was outside the entrance to my condo when the elevator door opened. There was an exasperated look on his face that said, screwed again by another deadbeat. I sprinted toward him digging into my purse for my billfold and the cash. A healthy tip put a better expression on his face.

Effie arrived a short while later, and as usual, the three of us gathered at the dining room table to discuss the day's events. The smell of chicken, beef and shrimp drifted around the table as we swapped containers and filled our plates. Effie and Aaron reached for chopsticks—I grabbed a fork. We talked between bites.

Aaron and I covered every detail for Effie. If we took a breath, she leaned forward with "what happened next" body language. Neither of us needed much prompting. The day was exciting and left us with unanswered questions.

I said, "Effie, see if you can put what happened in perspective. You may have a better view of it from the outside. I think I was too close to the action to make sense of it."

She left the table and returned from the kitchen with a bottle of White Zinfandel and three glasses. The neck of the bottle clinked against the wineglasses as she poured generous servings. We all settled back, sipping the wine.

Effie led the discussion. "We know Mr. Eberheart has access to the upper floors from his very own office. If he is involved, he has the perfect route to the tenth floor and back. If he killed Mr. Hawkins, he could have used it to escape from there after he pushed the man over the railing. I have two questions."

Aaron and I stared at her. I reached for the wine bottle and refilled my glass.

"Casey, you told us before you've heard someone up there. It must have been him. So, number one, if he killed Mr. Hawkins, why does he keep returning? And, number two—did he also kill Mr. Worthington?"

Aaron put a hand out, shaking an index finger. "Let's say Eberheart did the first dirty deed. He lost something up there during the murder. He's going back to find it because it could be incriminating."

Aaron poured more wine into his glass. I held mine out for another refill. He offered Effie more, but she put a hand on top of her glass.

"Makes sense," I said. "What did he lose?"

It was Effie's turn. "Could be clothing…or a monogrammed handkerchief. Could be something he wears…like eyeglasses. Could be…something from his clothes, like a lapel pin or a cufflink."

"I think I can rule out some of that," I said. "Eberheart doesn't wear glasses or cufflinks. Surely, someone would have noticed torn or missing clothing on him the day Hawkins died. I met him in his office the day Hawkins did the swan dive from…"

"What is it, Casey?" Aaron said.

"It wasn't missing clothing I saw the day Hawkins died, but there was white dust on the sleeve of his jacket—construction dust. He's not much of a fashion plate, and the dust was still on his coat even later the same day. He was up there, I'll bet my last dollar he killed Hawkins."

Effie said, "Then what is he looking for on the tenth floor? What could he have dropped?"

The three of us mentally chewed on those facts for a few minutes. We all must have come up empty, because it was so quiet I could hear the others breathing. Aaron and I drained the last of the Zinfandel into our glasses.

"Maybe I could snoop around the Midtown Atrium Towers Building," Effie said. "I'm the only one the suspects don't know by sight."

"I don't like that idea," I said. "Not for now, but if we can't move our investigation along…it's something to keep in mind."

"Haven't we forgotten another aspect?" Effie said. "We haven't tied the second murder into what we know about the first."

Effie was getting good at the investigative process. When we were bogged down, she seemed to be the catalyst to get us moving again. We all tossed ideas around about Worthington's death. It was almost a given the two deaths were linked. Still no motive or clear-cut suspect we could hang it all on.

"If they are tied together," Aaron said. "I think we already have our suspect. I don't think we have to look any farther than Eberheart. If he did the first one, it seems logical to me he did the second one. Only question in my mind is why he killed another Cyber-Technology employee."

That set off another flurry of debate, which was no more productive than the last one. We tended to agree with Aaron, but there were no definitive provable circumstances. "Why should we worry about that?" I said. "We don't have anything we could take to court to prove Eberheart did the first one, let alone Worthington."

Effie looked at me and said, "I bet if we can figure out what Mr. Eberheart is looking for at the murder scene, we could take it to Dennis and he would believe us."

"I bet you're right," I said. "And speaking of Dennis, who's going to give me some ideas about dinner for him tomorrow night?"

Raised eyebrows all around. I brought them up to speed about my anticipated date.

Aaron said, "Can you afford the gal who 'catered' for you last week?"

"I can afford her, but I'd be embarrassed to tell her how last week blew up in my face."

Effie and Aaron slipped out to the kitchen. I could hear whispered dialogue and giggles. When some of it turned to guffaws, I had to see what they were up to. In the kitchen, I found the two of them displaying a list of ingredients to me.

"We've got most of the items you'll need on this list," Aaron said.

Effie said, "We'll go out tomorrow morning and buy what's missing."

"Before we leave tomorrow," Aaron said. "We'll put it together so all you have to do is heat and serve."

Before I dropped off to sleep, I felt the warm glow again. I pictured myself in the kitchen and Dennis in the dining room. Then I saw myself delivering a feast to the table. The warm glow could have been from the wine, but it wasn't in my head—it was a good foot and a half further south.

33

SUNLIGHT SLASHED THROUGH THE CRACK IN THE drapes where I'd done a bad job of closing them. It dashed across the corner of my bed and spilled onto my pillow. Even with my eyes closed, it was more than a person should have to bear at this time of day. I ventured a peek, with one eye, to determine what time it was. Nine-thirty. Most of the day was still ahead of me.

A couple of aspirins and the toothbrush eased the wine throb in my head. I knew one of Effie's scrumptious omelets or French toast à la Aaron would take care of the rest of my morning problems.

Utter disappointment. The kitchen was bare, save a note from the two of them. They were off to the market and some specialty shops gathering the ingredients for the dinner I would serve Dennis tonight. I satisfied my hunger with a bowl of Cheerios.

They returned before noon. By then I'd showered and dressed in at-home casual. They shoo-ed me out of the kitchen telling me all was under control and I would have detailed instructions for preparing and serving the meal.

"I'm going to drop Effie at the bus station," Aaron said. He was standing near the front door, a gym bag near his feet.

My wristwatch said one-fifteen. "That was quick."

Effie rounded the corner from her bedroom with a backpack. She handed me the list of my duties and they both wished me luck. I was alone—until seven o'clock when Dennis was due to put in his appearance.

I settled into my favorite reading position, twisted sideways in my over-stuffed chair with my legs over the arm. The floor lamp behind the chair threw plenty of light on my reading material.

Wow, I thought. Every detail one could imagine was covered in their instructions, from: Seven, welcome Dennis. Seven-ten, hang up his coat and offer glass of wine. Seven-twenty, serve wine. In between those two notes was the name and location of the wine bottle chilling in the fridge. The list continued and told me what to put in the oven and when, and how to get it to the table in one piece. It went on and on until the final entry which read, "Nine forty-five, bedroom (on your own)." There was a smiley face drawn in the margin by that one.

By mid-afternoon, I'd gone over the list a half dozen times—practicing moving the various dishes around the kitchen. I figured I was ready for anything.

In my bedroom, I went into the walk-in closet. What should I wear? I asked the question to myself over and over. What atmosphere and mood did I want to project? Hard to get? Sexy? Easy? Ready? Ready for what, I thought.

Figuring it was the easiest, I went for sexy first. The third outfit was a black sheath—short, short with spaghetti straps. I checked myself in the full-length mirror and shook my head. "I don't think I can pull this one off," I said to the face staring back at me from the mirror. "First of all, the thin straps on the dress didn't cover the wide ones on my bra, and I didn't have a strapless. I considered braless and discarded the idea for lack of nerve rather than a lack of capability. "Maybe I better start with the basics." I stripped off everything and stepped in front of the mirror again.

"Not too bad," the lady in the mirror said to me. "A little bit of tummy, but all in all, not bad at all." Time on the treadmill and jogging was keeping me a step and a half ahead of Mother Time. "Give her some credit too. We don't want to be sexist, do we?"

Something in the mirror moved. I jumped and turned around. "Damn you, PK. Don't go sneaking up on me like a vulture." I did a full fashion runway turn for him and said, "What do you think? The old gal's still got it, huh?" PK made one of those strange sounds of his. "Just like a man. Get out of here. Shoo." Instead of leaving the room, he streaked for the closet, leaped up on the lower shelf of the clothes racks and disappeared behind a row of slacks.

I selected a bra and panties from my dresser and slipped into the black bikinis. I don't own any thongs, thank you. I don't see any reason to pay for something that gives me a wedgie on its own. The bra was black as well, and I liked what it did for my breasts. That's a reasonable start for the sexy look, I thought. Should I continue in that vein or try for something a bit more subtle? The lady in the mirror refused to respond.

The dress I selected was a red wrap-around model with a plunging neckline. Not so low I was in danger of falling out, but it should get Dennis' attention. There was also a glimpse of thigh if I made the right movement. I decided against hose, so the red shoes were the last item needed to complete the impression I was looking for. I laid the dress, shoes and underwear on the bed. There was plenty of time to get ready, so a short nap was in order. I could get up by five, shower and dress way before Dennis arrived at seven.

* * *

When I rolled over, the clock told me there was an hour and a half to get ready. A short refresher course couldn't hurt. Wearing only my bathrobe, I did a quick trip through the kitchen with the prep list in hand.

Lounging in the tub gave me one of those warm glows I enjoy. I stood and rinsed under the shower. The blow dryer did quick work with my short hair. I took my time with my makeup and found a little less than half hour remained before Dennis was due to arrive. Slipping on my underwear, dress and shoes didn't take long. A couple of dabs of perfume in strategic spots and I was in the living room with fifteen minutes to spare. Now, I could wait and appear casual when Dennis arrived. I knew he would be on time and it would be easy to follow my list of instructions.

I was sitting on the couch tapping my foot and staring at the clock when the doorbell did ring—at seven-seventeen. Now, how the hell do I follow a timed list, which starts at seven when he's seventeen minutes late?

I put the best smile I could gather on my face and opened the door—after using the peephole to confirm it was Dennis on the other side.

"Here," he said extending a bottle of wine in my direction. "I thought we could have this with dinner."

Son-of-a-bitch, I thought. Here he is late—not a nice round fifteen minutes late—but seventeen minutes late. How the hell do I adjust my timeline instructions for seventeen stinking minutes? And, another bottle of wine. Where in the hell does it fit into my schedule?

Enough of this crap, I told myself. I twisted as I reached for the bottle. There was a smile on his face so I was sure his eyes caught the thigh I flashed. I said, "Thanks. I'll put it on ice. Come on in and make yourself at home."

The evening and the meal went well. I managed the adjustments for the late start and we were watching the upfront weather forecast on the ten o'clock news. I thought of the last item on the list—nine forty-five, off to bed. I checked my watch, ten oh two. That's nine forty-five plus seventeen.

"What the heck are you grinning about," Dennis said.

"I was thinking about a note Aaron left earlier."

That put me between a rock and a hard place. I wanted to go to bed with Dennis, but I was stuck for a good answer or plan of action. I was the rock and I hoped he was the hard spot. Before I could think, "Do you want to make love to me?" came out of my mouth.

He stood up, reached down to take my hand and said, "Yes."

I don't think we said much after that. For the most part, it was action. There was enough light coming in the window to see most everything. Standing by my bed, Dennis unfastened the tie on my wrap-around dress and I shrugged my shoulders. The dress slid to the floor. He reached down and unhooked the front-closure bra. That left me standing there in little more than high heels and a smile. He put his arms around me and we kissed. The embraces continued until I got his shirt and T-shirt off. I unfastened his belt and his trousers dropped to the floor.

There was some squirming as I figured he was kicking out of his shoes and pants. He scooped me up in his arms and we collapsed onto the bed. Not one of the slow motion, smooth actions they put in the movies. It was more of a plop, and it brought a giggle from both of us. He reached down and took off his socks and as he rolled over to me, his shorts came off too.

The glow was spreading and so was the kissing. Dennis put his lips on my nipples. I put my fingers in his hair doing my best to guide his head and improve his aim. He slid his hand down my belly and inside my panties. I kicked my shoes off as he slid the panties down my legs.

I was ready to—couple, join, go at it, screw—whatever they were calling it these days. Dennis rose up a bit, kissed my mouth, then he reached over the side of the bed and retrieved his trousers. He's leaving, I thought. What the hell did I do wrong?

34

"WHAT'S THE MATTER?" I SAID.

Dennis' hand was in a pants pocket. "I'm getting some protection."

"Protection for what?" He pulled a condom from the pocket and I said, "Oh."

"I figured I'd wear something."

"Why? You think I've got something contagious?"

"No, I just…I just thought…Isn't that what they do today?"

I cussed myself. Too much time. Too much talk. I could see his manhood wilting. I reached out, put my hands on his shoulders and pulled him down next to me. That last question told me he's been as inactive on the sex scene as I have. I propped myself up on one elbow and said, "Maybe we should get the cob webs out of the closets before we consummate this…this arrangement."

I smiled and saw a grin spreading across his face before he buried it in a pillow.

We were in each other's arms stifling laughter—and not doing a good job of it.

"Who wants to go first?" Dennis said.

I didn't want to, but I said, "Oh, what the hell." I covered my relationship with Jarvis the Rat.

Fourteen years married. Only the second man I ever slept with. When the divorce came up, I asked Jarvis how many women there had been. He swore Bambi was the first one. He swore he and Bambi were clean and there was no reason to be afraid of any diseases. There was no reason not to believe him except for the betrayal and hatred I felt. That did nothing to assuage my paranoia. "I went for the blood tests every two months for the first year," I told Dennis. "Since then, I've gotten a six-month check and I'm about due for another. According to the labs, I'm clean."

It took several minutes before Dennis screwed up enough courage to tell his story. "I was engaged. She wasn't the first woman I slept with, but when she came along, she was the only one. We were engaged for almost four years—living together for the last year and a half. She died…drunk driver…never had a chance…she was dead in her car. I was working, heard the accident call and rolled up on the scene. I recognized her car…I couldn't believe what I was seeing."

Dennis took several deep breaths and turned his head away from me. He told me she died four years ago. And only in the last year did he begin to think about going out with someone. "I was concerned about the dating thing, so I got a couple of blood tests. The lab gave me a clean bill of health too."

I snuggled closer to him and he seemed to relax. He looked at me and we embraced.

"Don't we still need some protection…? You know, for the pregnancy thing?"

"I take care of that. Considering I haven't been with a man since Jarvis and I split, that's a lot of wasted birth control pills."

The humor didn't escape either of us. We were still laughing when he drew me closer. We wrapped arms and legs around each other and relaxed. We were too relaxed. I awoke in the middle of the night and we were still close, but nothing relating to sex occurred. The next thing I became aware of was sunlight streaming in the window to my room. I was alone.

* * *

I rolled out of bed and started for the bathroom. I kicked my shoes toward the closet, grabbed my dress, bra and panties and tossed them into the hamper. I didn't see any of Dennis' clothes. "Son-of-a-bitch," I said as I stalked to the vanity. The toothpaste did wonders for my mouth, but not a thing to improve my humor.

I rose up and looked at myself in the mirror. How the hell could he pass up this body? A movement in the mirror startled me and I thought it was PK again. It wasn't. Dennis was grinning at me and holding two cups of coffee.

"I thought this would help to wake us both up," he said.

He was wearing his pants, and I assumed his under shorts, but no shoes or shirt. Looking down at myself in the mirror again, I said, "I need a robe."

We sat on the bed sipping coffee and talking. I didn't want to break the mood, but sometime in the future I would have to ask Dennis about a couple of scars he carried. There was a little round one on his left chest and a rather jagged and nasty three-inch healed wound on his rib cage.

"I enjoyed last night," he said.

"Me too."

"Sorry it ended like it did, but at least I didn't have to face performance anxiety."

I smiled at him. "From what I saw, you wouldn't have any problem in that regard." He looked a little surprised.

"You think girls don't look at bodies?" He still didn't say anything. "Dennis, you're blushing."

"I thought as much." He leaned over and kissed me.

"Would you like to pick up where we left off last night?" I couldn't believe I was being that bold. Not typical of me, but I liked the guy.

"Sounds like fun, but I'm on call at noon and it's more than likely I'll get paged."

I grabbed a small note pad from the bedside table. I wrote "rain," added a checkmark by it and held it up to Dennis. He smiled and I tucked the rain check between my breasts inside the robe. "You'll have to retrieve it if you plan to use it."

He kissed me again and slid his hand into the robe. When he leaned back, he held the note up to me and winked.

Dennis puttered around in the kitchen and we ate a light brunch. He wasn't very handy at food prep, but he was still better than I am.

He was right about his work. At eleven-thirty his cell phone rang. He muttered a couple of "Okays" into the phone and ended the call. "Gotta go, damn it. Duty calls," he said. I escorted him to the door where we shared a long goodbye kiss. After I closed the door, I watched him through the peep hole until he disappeared.

The rest of the day on my own centered on reading the Sunday newspaper and doing some housework. That fooled me. I don't know what set off the domesticity in me, but I washed dishes and dusted the living room.

The phone rang at eight p.m. Dennis and I spent an hour and a half jabbering. I felt like a teenager. He said goodbye telling me it was time for him to get back to work. He also broke the news he would be on eleven-to-seven's for the next two weeks. When I asked what that meant, he said it was the late evening to early morning shift. There goes sex for the time being, I thought.

* * *

Effie got home at noon on Labor Day and Aaron followed a couple of hours later. They talked about their weekend visits and I thanked them for their efforts that made Saturday night dinner a success.

Effie asked about Dennis, and I evaded details. I spent a lot of time covering dinner but little about the after-hours activities.

We all headed for bed early. On the way out of the living room, Aaron whispered to me, "You two didn't sleep together, did you?"

"Well…we were together…and we did sleep." I knew I was turning red.

Aaron winked and said, "Don't sweat it. It'll happen soon enough."

35

I MADE IT TO WORK AN HOUR BEFORE MY USUAL start time on Tuesday morning. Cheryl needed to know Eberheart came back to the office Friday afternoon. I didn't want her to get caught short if he questioned her.

I took a seat outside the cafe. Someone left a newspaper on the table and I kept glancing at it. I nearly missed Cheryl when she entered the lobby. My wild arm waving caught her eye and she came over and sat down. I covered the Friday details for her.

"Oh, my God. Now Mr. Eberheart will know I left early. I'm dead meat."

"Whoa, gal. Here's your story. You went to the restroom somewhere around four forty-five and locked the front door to C-T. You didn't want anyone wandering in. He must have come by while you were in the bathroom."

"How about you? Won't he wonder why you didn't come to the front door?"

"If he does ask about me, tell him you don't know and he should ask me. By the time he gets around to checking, I'll have a CD player and a headset in my desk." I patted my purse. "I'll say he didn't knock loud enough for me to hear over the music."

She took a few minutes to think about the story and apparently thought she could pull it off. "How do you think of all these things?"

"I guess I just have a devious nature," I said with a smile and a wink. "Go on up to the office. I'll be there in a few minutes."

Cheryl walked toward the elevators and I sipped my coffee. Eberheart came into view—I couldn't be sure from where. I wondered if he saw me with Cheryl and held the newspaper up in front of my face. I peeked around the paper, and he didn't look my direction. He did quicken his step so he could catch up with her. They got into the same elevator. I sensed some relief, but held my breath for Cheryl.

In the office I played it cool and didn't go near Cheryl. I did slip her a note on one of my many trips back and forth.

Cheryl trailed me by a few minutes for the morning break. We found a table in the lobby and she couldn't contain herself. She leaned as far across the table as she could and whispered, "You're a true life saver. Mr. Eberheart cornered me in the elevator and took me to his office as soon as we got up to Cyber-Tech. I think he believed the story you gave me. He even asked me about you. Did he ask you why you didn't hear him?"

I shook my head and steered the conversation to her long weekend. That was a mistake. I wanted to get around to Eberheart as the subject, but there wasn't time left. I got the quick and dirty version of her escapades—she was a hell of a lot luckier than I was Saturday night—and we made a date for lunch to complete the details.

Cheryl headed for the elevators, and before I could get up from the table, Dennis appeared from across the lobby. He sat down with me. "I'm on my way home from work. Wanted to see you."

I related my tale of exploring the utility shaft on Friday with Aaron and of our escape from Eberheart.

"When the hell were you planning on telling me about that—about putting yourself in danger?"

"I could have told you Saturday, but there were more important things on my mind. I planned on telling you about it—about now." He didn't seem to care for my attempt at humor. We went over the possibilities of Eberheart being the killer, but we were still stuck for a motive for the second murder.

"How about I come back at noon so we can discuss this further?"

"Make it early, maybe eleven-thirty. I've got a date with Cheryl from my office. I want to get her take on Eberheart."

* * *

Over a tuna salad sandwich and iced tea, Dennis and I went over everything we knew about the case. He thought the fraud was enough to trigger the killings. "Do you think all the guys in your office were in on the computer break-ins and fraud?"

"They each operated in their own specialty and there didn't seem to be much in the way of cross training. I think at least the three main players, Harmon, Eberheart and Worthington would of necessity be involved. Then there are the shadowy characters dropping in and out Cheryl told me about." I made a mental note to see if she could identify my attacker from the composite image of him.

"How's this for a what-if?" he said. "Hawkins learned Cyber-Technology stole some internal information from Bon-eventure and sold it to a competitor. He tells Eberheart he's going to blow the whistle on C-T. Eberheart kills Hawkins. Worthington suspects Eberheart is responsible for Hawkins' death and is getting cold feet. Eberheart decides to toss him over the tenth floor railing as well."

"Works for me. How do we prove it?"

"Looks to me like we could have the motive—how about opportunity?"

Dennis looked up like he was reviewing some information in his mind's eye. "Almost everyone in the building we've talked to has the same type situation. Everyone was with someone and they give each other an alibi. Like your guys—Harmon and Eberheart were working together when Hawkins and Worth-ington died."

"Does that get them off the hook?"

"Not really. They have an alibi, but it's about the weakest one they could have."

I looked up and saw Cheryl stop about half-way across the lobby. She seemed hesitant to approach me since I was with someone. I waved her over. Before she got to the table, I asked Dennis if he wanted to come to dinner Saturday night. He nodded a vigorous yes.

I introduced Cheryl to Dennis. I referred to him as a boy-friend, with a wink and a grin, and omitted the fact he was a detective. I didn't think she would remember him from the days of the murders. "Dennis was about to leave."

He took the not-so-subtle hint and excused himself, saying, "I'll give you a call tonight."

My deception seemed to work. Cheryl didn't give any indication she recognized Dennis. She dashed through the cafeteria line and was back sitting across from me in a few minutes. "I've got to thank you again," she said. "I know I would have fallen apart when Mr. Eberheart cross-examined me if you hadn't given me a good story line."

I was glad she was appreciative, because I was about to lay some heavy duty questions on her. I eased the likeness of my attacker out of my purse. "Cheryl, does this look like anyone you've seen before?"

She unfolded the paper and studied it, then put it face down on the table. Cheryl turned in her chair so I couldn't see her face and said, "I don't think so."

Her voice was low enough it didn't come near convincing me. "Are you sure you don't know him?" I didn't give her much room. "Cheryl?"

"I think he's one of our employees who doesn't come around much."

"The ones you told me about before?" I said.

She nodded, put her head down and concentrated on her salad. I pushed her to take another look and she confirmed he was a C-T employee. I needed to get the records on the guy, but I'd never seen any employee files on anyone except the folks who showed up regularly. "Do you know where Mr. Harmon keeps their files?"

Cheryl kept her head down shoveling in the lettuce, so I tried a different subject. "What do you think about Mr. Eberheart? Is he really the one in control at Cyber-Technology?"

She was quiet for a long time, then, "I don't want to talk about him…he scares me."

When I asked what scared her, she told me there was something in his eyes that put her on edge. It happened more than once. The worst time was when he was talking to Worthington—a couple of days before he died. "You know," Cheryl said, "sometimes they talk about a look that could kill. Mr. Eberheart's got that look—he scares me."

36

I TOOK A LATE-AFTERNOON BREAK BECAUSE DENNIS called and wanted to stop by again. That was his third time to see me today and I asked him when he planned to get some sleep.

"I grabbed a couple of hours this afternoon. I'll get by."

We spent twenty minutes going over the same ground we'd covered this morning and at noon. We got no further than before; the suspicions and motives were still there and were still tenuous. He was interested in the fact that my attacker did some kind of work for Cyber-Tech, but there was nowhere to go with the information until they could ID him.

"I found out I'll only be on nights for about a week," Dennis said. "Could I prevail on you not to do any more sleuthing until I'm around during the daytime?"

"What's the matter? 'fraid I'll break the case before you do?"

He smiled but I was sure he was worried.

I went back to my office and got everything ready for the next day. Taking my break so late didn't leave much room until going-home time. The big hand pointed straight down, so I retrieved my purse from the desk drawer. I took a moment to complete my time card for the day.

"Where the hell have you been?"

Eberheart's voice startled me. "What do you mean by that?"

"I came by here around four-fifteen and you weren't here."

He was beginning to piss me off. "I took a late break this afternoon." He took a step back.

"I don't care for your tone of voice. You never seem to be at your desk."

"I take a fifteen-minute break in the morning and the afternoon and an hour for lunch—all of which I'm entitled to, and I take them. If you have a complaint with my work or my work habits, I suggest you take it up with Mr. Harmon."

I waited for a reply, which didn't come. I stood, stuck my watch in Eberheart's face and said "It's after five-thirty and I'm on my own time. Unless you have something else, I'll leave now."

"Do you ever wander around other floors?"

That one came close to jerking the rug out from under me. I snorted and slung my bag over my shoulder. "This floor and the lobby are about all I've seen in this building." I didn't wait for another question. I pushed by him and left the C-T offices. I made it to the elevator before my knees began to shake.

* * *

Aaron was off on another overnighter, leaving Effie and me to solve the world's problems. At the sound of my name, I pulled my nose out of my mystery novel.

"Casey, I've been thinking about my hair again."

PK made one of his wild dashes across the room, leapt for the table in the wall mural, hit and slid to the floor. A couple of those "come here" kissey noises and he ambled over to me. I looked at Effie. "What are you thinking about doing?"

"I want it shorter. Could you call the friend you told me about and go with me?"

I told her I'd contact Terry in the morning and see if she could work us in on Saturday. "How short do you want it?"

"I think you were right. I'd better not go as short as yours is. Maybe up off my neck. Do you think I would look good as a blond like you?"

"That may be too much of a change. I think Terry could add highlights and make it a lot lighter."

We spent some time talking about the details Dennis discussed with me during the day. Effie agreed with the basic premise Eberheart was the most likely suspect. She fussed at me when I told her about standing up to him tonight before I left the office. She had a point when she said he might be trying to bait me into admitting I was investigating the killings. "I'll keep my distance from him," I said.

37

THE FIRST THING WEDNESDAY MORNING I MADE A hair appointment for Effie. We would have to be there by seven a.m. Since Terry was doing me a big favor on short notice, I didn't figure I could complain.

Much of my time today was spent dodging Eberheart. Every time he came around the corner toward my cubicle, I located something I needed to take to Harmon's office. A number of bathroom breaks cut him off at the pass as well. It got to be a real game playing cat and mouse with him. Except—I wasn't sure who was the feline and who was the rodent.

He's about the only thing on my mind when I wasn't busy on the computer getting C-T's bills paid and deposits ready.

At noon, I pumped Cheryl again about the Cyber-Tech staff. She was still nervous about identifying the picture of my assailant as an employee. Of course, she had no idea he assaulted me. I wondered how worried she would be if she knew what he did. In her mind, Eberheart still seemed to be more of a boss than Wayne Harmon.

Cheryl left early and I sat there in the lobby café looking up at the interior walls of the atrium. My mind wandered from Dennis to the murders and then back to Dennis again. Kind of a one-track mind. I did my best to relive the last Saturday night—this time with a better ending. I could almost feel his hot skin on mine—and the glow was moving from my mind down to my toes—and all the spots in between.

I found myself staring up at the tenth floor balcony when something hit me. I sat bolt upright, my mind leaping from issue to issue. That something was on the tip of my brain, but I couldn't bring it into focus. Dennis…or something Dennis said…or something I saw? It remained fuzzy, so I gave up on it following the old adage: don't concentrate on remembering and it will come to you.

I relaxed and spent the balance of my lunch hour people-watching. When my time was up and the coffee cold, I went back up to my office. Despite warnings from Dennis and the interest Eberheart was showing in me, I planned to snoop around the building some more, so I called home hoping Aaron was back and would answer the phone.

No luck. Aaron must have stopped off somewhere before returning. I had a plan and I needed his expertise. I phoned home again and that time I left a message on the machine.

Aaron returned my call in mid-afternoon. "I need you to pick a lock for me," I said.

"What kind of lock?"

I told him it was a door to the utility shaft like the one in Eberheart's office. "…except these are the ones on ten, eleven and twelve."

"Why do you need them open?"

"I plan to take another look around up there. The tenth floor is calling again. I know there is something we've missed. And I want escape routes."

"Escape from what?"

There was a sound of concern in Aaron's voice so I told him about my further run-in's with Eberheart. "I think it would be prudent to have more than one way out."

"I think it would be wise," he said, "if you lay off the prowling around altogether. Didn't Dennis ask you to do that even before this last confrontation?"

"Just come here this afternoon and block those doors open for me. I promise I won't do anything until we talk about it. We can do that at home tonight."

Aaron didn't sound enthusiastic, but promised he would do the job. He also said I wouldn't see him since he was concerned, and he didn't want Eberheart to put the two of us together. Aaron reminded me Eberheart saw him when we gave him the slip on the tenth floor.

* * *

My two partners in crime and I enjoyed a good meal—Effie was still the culinary whiz of the group. Aaron described what he accomplished that afternoon. "I found several magnetic strips like your name badge," he said. "I picked the lock on the door to the utility shaft and installed a strip that'll let you get through."

"Which floor?" Effie said.

Aaron smiled. "All of them. You can get into the shaft from twelve, or eleven or ten."

Effie said, "You've been a busy bee, Aaron. Casey, when do I get to do something else to help the investigation?"

"I still need your logic to help put everything in perspective."

Effie frowned. "You know that's not what I'm asking about. I want to go to the building and snoop around like you're doing. I bet I could find something there."

"I'd be too worried about you," I said. "I'm going to start taking my gun along with me—in my purse. I've got one made for a concealed weapon."

That drew a frown from both of them.

I went to my room and retrieved the gun and two magazines for it. They each hold ten rounds and I slid one into the butt of the Glock. I put the weapon and spare magazine into my handbag.

The phone rang and I hoped it was Dennis. It was. He wasn't the least bit thrilled when I told him the Glock was installed in my special handbag.

"That's a lousy idea, Casey. I'm asking you to leave the gun at home."

"If I'd known how you'd react, I wouldn't have mentioned it. I took a lot of training with handguns and—"

"Damn it, Casey. Have you ever pointed a gun at a human being? It's a damn sight different than shooting at paper targets."

"Hold on a minute. I've been through a tactical shooting course, and—"

"Fine. How many of the silhouettes on the course were shooting back? I'll repeat my first question. Have you ever pointed your gun at a real person?"

"Well…no. But I think I can do it."

"Thinking don't feed the bulldog. If you draw your weapon and point it at somebody, you'd better be ready to pull the trigger and kill them. If you don't, they'll walk right up to you, jerk the gun out of your hand and put a big nasty hole right in your middle. Take it from the voice of experience, you won't like the feeling of a gunshot wound—they hurt like hell and you bleed all over your clothes."

I pictured the round scar on the left side of Dennis' chest near the shoulder. He was worried about me and I liked his interest. I didn't need him to be overbearing. "I appreciate your concern," I said. "I'll put your admonitions at the top of the list." Topic shift, I thought. "How much longer are you going to be on night duty?"

"Looks like I should be back on days by the first of next week."

"That sounds good. Maybe some evening we could pick up where we left off last weekend." The silence lasted longer than I wanted it to. I wondered if he was getting cold feet. "Or, maybe we could try for a nooner before you go back on days." I couldn't believe what I was saying. The words expressed the desires, but I seldom talked about sex and never was that bold or forward.

"Ah…I'm sleeping around noontime…"

Oh, damn. I'm scaring him away, or there's no interest left.

"Casey, I know I can't talk you out of carrying the gun, but please think about what I said. It's an old saw, but still sensible.

If push comes to shove, you can't afford to hesitate…better to be judged by twelve than carried by six."

"I will. I'll hang up now and let you go to work."

I sat on the edge of the bed thinking about Dennis and me rolling around in the sheets. We came close to making love in a room with enough moonlight streaming in the window we were visible to one another. That wasn't like me any more than the words I spoke to Dennis. I don't think I saw as much of Jarvis until we'd been married for years. I preferred the dark and never talked about what we were doing. Actually, what Jarvis was doing. I didn't provide any input—I wonder if that was part of our problem.

I fell asleep with those thoughts swirling through my head.

38

THE SAME VISIONS WERE SCURRYING AROUND IN MY head when I awoke. I thought about what I'd said to Dennis—big, bold and brassy. Except that wasn't like me. Was I trying to be someone he would be attracted to? Or, was I doing my best to scare him off?

"I guess I won't know until I decide what my feelings for him really are."

I also better keep my thoughts in my head rather than voicing them out loud.

Two more weekdays and the weekend until Dennis should be back on day shifts. Then I could resume my extra-curricular activities at the Midtown Atrium Towers Building. After all, a promise is a promise.

I beat Effie to the kitchen, which surprised me. Little Miss Perfect—late. Meow, I thought. No need to be catty. Most of our breakfast fare, cold cereal, was on the kitchen table when Effie made an appearance.

"Sorry," she said. "I think my alarm clock died during the night."

We ate and the next time I saw her was at the front door—ready to leave for work—on time.

She looked serious. "Do you have time to drop me at work?"

I told her I could handle it. By the time we were settled into the Mustang she began, "I'm getting left behind. I did most of the research that led us to the fraud by Cyber-Technology. You asked Aaron to go to the MAT building twice to help you."

She was squirming in her seat as she spoke. I could tell she was uncomfortable talking to me like that. I also figured she felt hurt for being sidelined.

"Casey, if you don't want me to help you anymore, just say so. If not, maybe I'll figure out a way I can do it on my own."

"Right now there isn't much we can do." I told her about my promise to Dennis. "When we go at it again, I'll be sure you're included."

She seemed satisfied with my explanation, and I dropped her at her office in the Hillcrest area. Rather than taking Markham Street to downtown, I decided to use Cantrell Road. I picked it up in an area of beautiful older homes where the trees formed a shaded arch over the street and moderated the temperature. Later, it would give me a reasonable view of the Arkansas River. I swung by the back side of the Doubletree and Peabody Hotels, and took the sharp right bend where the road became Cumberland Street and dumped me into the downtown area.

* * *

I was thinking about taking my morning break when I noticed Eberheart coming down the hall in his shirt sleeves. He seldom went without a jacket. We passed without saying a word. With no jacket, I noticed something, which wasn't usually visible. I almost stopped dead in my tracks. My breath was coming in short gulps. My knees were weak. I needed to get somewhere to run the facts over in my mind.

His voice came from behind me. "Don't cross me, Fremont," Eberheart said. "I can guarantee you don't want me as an enemy."

I pretended I didn't hear him and kept walking. I made it to the elevator and slumped into a back corner. The ride was interminable. It felt like we stopped at every floor to take on and discharge passengers. By the time we descended to the lobby level, my knees were steady again and I felt like I could release the bar I'd been clutching for the full ride down.

I grabbed a quick cup of coffee and took it to a small table off to the side of the lobby. I wanted to be by myself. I thought about seeing Eberheart in the office. No jacket. Shirt sleeves rolled half way up to the elbow. His C-T identification badge swinging back and forth across his shirt front as he walked. My eyes bored in on the chain the ID badge hung from—a beaded chain. As soon as I saw it, I remembered Dennis detailing the personal effects taken from the body of Hawkins—a beaded chain.

When was it Eberheart came to me for a replacement badge? I couldn't remember for sure, but I believed it was shortly after Hawkins died. I could check my files for the exact date when I returned to the office. Never mind for now, I thought. The image was forming in my mind. I could see Eberheart wrestling Hawkins toward the balcony railing. Hawkins is struggling—grabbing at anything that could save him. His hand finds the chain of Eberheart's ID badge and Hawkins rips it from Eberheart's neck. Hawkins goes over the railing still clutching it.

That would explain how the chain was still in Hawkins' possession when he hit the lobby floor. Question: Where is Eberheart's old ID badge? It didn't show up in the lobby. The police didn't find anything on the tenth floor—unless they somehow missed it. If they missed it—it was still up there.

And like the light bulb coming on over the head of a cartoon character, I knew what Eberheart's visits to the tenth floor were all about. The police did miss the badge, and it was still there. He was trying to find it, because it could tie him to the scene where Hawkins started his swan dive.

I was sitting so my knees weren't shaky, but my hand was. Half-way to my mouth, the coffee cup was quivering to the extent I was afraid to take a sip. I needed to share it with someone, so I got my cell phone from my purse. I tried my home, but Aaron wasn't there. I called Effie's office and asked her to call me back on her cell.

I bounced the scenario off Effie. She sounded excited. "Casey, I think you're on the right track. Have you told anyone else?"

After what she'd said that morning on the ride to work, I was ashamed to say I'd phoned Aaron first. Since he wasn't home when I called, I wasn't lying when I said, "No, you're the first."

"I think you should tell Dennis as soon as you can."

My watch told me he'd been in bed a couple of hours at most. "I'll call him this afternoon. I want the three of us, you, Aaron and me, to go through all of this tonight."

By noontime I was starving, but decided to make a pass through the tenth floor on my way to the lobby. It was out of the way, drawing me like a magnet. I took the stairs from nine to twelve and used the ladders to get back down to ten. By now crime scene tape didn't slow me down. I worked my way around the area where the bodies began their trip to the lobby floor. I stood there picturing the struggle between Hawkins and Eberheart. They are scuffling, turning, Mr. Hawkins grabbing for something, which will help him. He grabs the chain, Eberheart shoves him over the railing. Hawkins takes the broken chain with him and Eberheart's badge goes…where? My eyes swept the area in ever increasing circles from the center of the crime scene. Nothing. Except a stack of metal wall studs about ten feet back from the railing where Hawkins spent the last seconds of his life.

The police searched that pile. I've even looked around there. I started toward the stack when someone back in the darkness made a sound. The voice boomed—it was Eberheart. "What the hell are you doing up here?"

He was coming from the door to the utility shaft. What's the best escape route? I wheeled and retreated. The door to the stairwell was the closest and in the opposite direction from him. I bolted through the door and took the stairs to nine. Grabbing my magnetic bar from the ninth floor door jam, I headed to the restroom where I checked my clothes for telltale signs.

I emerged from the bathroom and found Eberheart standing in the hall. I didn't think he could have seen my face up there.

The lighting where I was standing wasn't the best, but he must have gotten a general image of me.

"Where the hell have you been? I looked for you at your desk and you were gone again, Fremont."

I hate it when they do that. Why can't they be polite enough to call me "Ms." or use my first name? "Didn't know I had to check with you when I went to take a pee." His face turned red, but he didn't say anything. I walked past him and was amazed my knees supported me. I took the elevator to the lobby. I felt the need to get away, so I went for lunch at the River Market.

39

I SPENT THE BALANCE OF THE DAY STEERING CLEAR of Eberheart. My work load was still light and didn't take up much of my time. That gave me an even better opportunity to think about him and how to keep out of his way. I put in several calls to Dennis; no answer so I left a voice mail message for him.

Getting out of the office and heading for home took a load off my shoulders. I looked forward to kicking off my shoes and relaxing with my roomies over a glass of wine.

* * *

When dinner was out of the way, we poured the wine and began our discussions. I explained my encounter with Eberheart and his questions. Effie asked how I got away and what doors were rigged to give me an advantage.

A discussion of motives was filled with animation and loud voices. Wild arm waving attempts to out-shout the others became the order of the evening.

Aaron waved his arms the best—like counter-rotating propellers—so we gave him the floor. "I think we're right-on about the reasons Hawkins was killed. I'm not sure about Worthington. Would these guys kill one of their own employees?"

I leaped to my feet. "If you could see the looks Eberheart gives me, you might consider that a pointless question." I also told them of Cheryl's comment about being scared by him.

Effie stood and waved both arms over her head in a serpentine parody of the two of us. "If you ask me," she said, "I think it's a logical conclusion the two deaths are connected. In my opinion, Mr. Worthington didn't agree with the killing of Mr. Hawkins. He may have gone along with the fraud and then tried to back away from what it led to."

I needed to study Effie's demeanor because she got to speak her mind with humor and without shouting. This lady is sharp, I reminded myself again.

She said, "Tell me more about what you did to the doors." Aaron told her about the magnetic plates he used. She kept at it. "I'm having a problem picturing where they are. Which doors? Where are they, related to the ladder we used to get down to the tenth floor?"

Aaron got a legal pad and pencil from my desk. "I'm better with pictures. Here's the layout of the floors."

I watched as he sketched the floor plan, putting in the location of the utility shaft, the stairwell doors and the floor-to-floor ladders. "That's darn good, Aaron," I said. "Did you study architecture?"

"As a matter of fact I have. I'm still working on a degree... very slowly." He looked at Effie. "Do these drawings help put it in perspective?"

Effie nodded and offered a toast to his future success as the Frank Lloyd Wright of Little Rock. The discussion returned to the Midtown Atrium Towers Building.

We agreed on the motives for both murders. We also agreed Eberheart was the one we should be looking at. Then we tried to figure out how to go at him. It didn't seem like a direct approach would work. I doubted he would crumple when an accusing finger was pointed at him. He was more apt to strike out—like a wounded or cornered animal.

Lapsing into silence, we finished our wine. I retreated within myself and began to think about Dennis. Enough, I said to myself. It's time to think of someone else.

"Aaron," I said, "if you are taking courses, you need a place to study. You also need a drafting table and a place for it." He told me he could put classes on hold until he found a location for that kind of setup. "Don't wait any longer. This weekend, we'll rearrange the furniture in the computer room so you can have space to get on with your studies."

Aaron was beaming and I turned to Effie. "What kind of interests do you have that we need to make room for?"

"I'd like to have a sewing machine, but I could use my room… if you don't mind me bringing the stuff in."

"I almost forgot about Saturday. We'll have to wait until after Effie's hair appointment to do the shuffling. I know some folks where we might find the gear you both need."

"What are you going to do with your hair?" Aaron said.

She explained what was on her mind. Aaron kept nodding like a brother approving his little sister's plans.

I said, "Aaron, if you want to come along—it shouldn't take too long—we can get an early start on the shopping Saturday morning as soon as we leave the beauty shop."

Aaron agreed. We poured another glass of wine for each of us and toasted the upcoming weekend.

40

TGIF. IT WAS A QUIET MORNING AND I ARRIVED AT work on time. I didn't see Eberheart around and hoped he was out for the day. I was getting tired of dodging him.

Cheryl and I took a morning break together. I kept the topics light and got another run-down on the previous weekend's adventures. I did ask a few questions, looking for tips I could apply to my own love life, or lack thereof. We were about to start back for the C-T offices when my cell phone rang. It was Aaron.

"I have to cancel tomorrow's day out with the girls," he said. The grin on his face was obvious in his voice. "I got a call from work. An attendant got sick and they need a warm body for today. It's a short out-and-back, so I'll be home by tomorrow afternoon."

I told him we could reschedule the trip to get the drafting table and we hung up. The rest of the day was as quiet as the earlier part.

* * *

Effie and I arrived at Terry's beauty shop a few minutes before seven a.m. on Saturday morning. Terry is a whiz with hair and can turn a tangled mane into a thing of splendor. Effie was no exception. That's not to say her hair was a mess—it was plain and she needed help.

Terry's scissors were a blur as she clipped a couple of inches off Effie's hair. The highlights Terry added fit Effie and the overall effect was fantastic. I think the smile on Effie's face said it all.

"How much do I owe you?" Effie said.

Terry gave her a figure. Effie looked pleased and pulled several bills from her purse. "It does sound awful reasonable."

"That includes the Casey discount," Terry said. "Casey and all her friends are entitled to the special rate."

Outside the shop, Effie asked about the reduced fee. "Does everybody in town owe you favors?"

"Not everyone. How about some breakfast?"

We stopped at a small restaurant in a strip mall on Rodney Parham. I asked Effie if she was ready to look for the sewing machine she mentioned.

"I'm not in the mood," she said. "I'd like to do some souvenir shopping for my family. Could you drop me around the River Market?"

"Want some company?"

"Don't think I'm not grateful, but I'd like to spend some time on my own. I can get a bus home…or take a cab."

I did what she asked, mentally shaking my head all the way into town. I wondered why, but it was her life to live.

Looking for a diversion of my own, I drove to Park Plaza Mall. A few hours in the clothing sections of several stores would put me in a good mood. A huge pretzel and fancy coffee drink would ruin my supper. Glancing around and not seeing my mother anywhere in sight, I went for it.

At home, the early get-up and busy shopping day caught up with me. PK began bugging me with loud meows as soon as I walked in, so I fed him. I lay down on the couch as soon as the chore was out of the way and fell asleep when my head hit the pillow.

* * *

The six p.m. news was on when Aaron returned. He described the weather and maintenance problems that delayed his flight back to Little Rock.

I told him I'd dropped Effie earlier and was wondering what was keeping her. "I've never known her to stay out on her own like this."

Aaron shrugged. "She's a big girl. I'm sure we'll hear from her before long."

As the first of the prime-time television shows came on, I looked over my shoulder at the answering machine. I forgot to check it when I came home. The Message Waiting light was blinking and I punched the button.

"I found it…"

It was Effie's voice and the time of the call was recorded at one this afternoon.

"What's she mean?" Aaron said.

I replayed the message and we listened to it again. "What the hell did she find?" I said. "She was trinket shopping for her family. Why would she call to tell us she found something?"

We stared at one another and I played it a third time. It didn't help, but we both said it sounded like she was cut off. We did our best to reassure each other. That wasn't helping, but at this point there didn't seem to be anything we could do.

"If she's not back by morning, I'm calling Dennis," I said.

41

I WAS UP AT FIVE A.M., WHICH IS WAY BEFORE MY usual get-up time. Aaron beat me. He was already in the kitchen with a pot of coffee sitting on the counter when I walked in.

Aaron said, "I checked the answering machine. Nothing new."

"I'm scared. What could Effie be up to? More to the point, what would keep her from letting us know what she was doing?"

"What bothers me is the message she left. I'm thinking she was telling us what she was doing…and she got interrupted."

"I tried Dennis, but he's out of the office and his cell phone must be turned off."

We chugged coffee for an hour, most of the time in silence. Aaron looked at his wrist watch. "Look, it's a little past six. A shower and the drive downtown and it'll be seven. I bet the weekend security guards will be on duty by then. We could at least nose around your office building."

"Do you think she went over there?"

Aaron shrugged his shoulders and said, "You got a better idea?"

Without another word, we both moved toward our rooms.

* * *

We beat Aaron's estimate—it was a little before seven when we arrived at the Midtown Atrium Towers Building. We peeked in the front door and waited until one of the two guards left the security desk before we entered. I told the remaining rent-a-cop I left my eyeglasses in our office on Friday. He said he couldn't leave the desk until his sidekick returned.

The weekend sign-in register was open on the counter. A bunch of eye rolls and head nods and Aaron got the hint. He reached over the counter, grabbed the guard's newspaper and whipped open the sports section. Before you could say, whatever, he gained the man's attention.

I ran my finger down the entries in the log, which was upside down to me—a trick I learned in another misspent vocation. Nothing of interest. I caught Aaron's eye and used my hands to let him know I wanted to turn the page of the book.

"Hey, look at this," Aaron said, shoving the paper across the counter toward the guard. When the newspaper blocked the view, I eased the page over and checked the previous day's entries. Aaron picked up my head nod and he wrapped up the sports talk and we headed for the front door.

Outside the building, he said, "What did you find?"

"About half-way down the Saturday page I found an entry for Eliza Doolittle. Next to her name in the TIME IN column was an entry reading '12 pm.' The matching TIME OUT spot was blank."

"So who the hell's Eliza Doolittle?"

I told him about thinking of Effie as the fictional Eliza. "I think she used the name as cover. She went in, but never came out."

I tried Dennis again and this time I got an answer at his house. He wasn't happy since I dragged him out of bed five minutes after he crawled in, a fact he related in a loud voice. I told him what we found and asked him to come to the MAT building so we could go in using his authority. "Can you get a search warrant by the time you get here?"

He was less than encouraging. "I hate to tell you this, Casey, but you don't have probable cause. I can't see a judge issuing a warrant. You don't have any real evidence."

"Are you coming or not?"

There was a long pause before Dennis answered. "I'll come down there, but it won't do much good. All the guard has to say is 'No' and I'm stymied."

* * *

We waited for Dennis across the street from my office building. I slammed an elbow into Aaron's ribs and I heard a gasp of air escape. "Look over there." I pointed to a man going into the MAT building. "That's Eberheart."

"I could try to follow him…and hope he didn't get a good a look at me the other day."

"I don't think we can chance it. I sure can't go over there. That would prove his suspicions about me. Where the hell is Dennis? Eberheart wouldn't recognize him."

We were OBE—overtaken by events. Eberheart disappeared inside while we stood there. "Hell," I said. "At least we can see what floor he goes to. You go down that direction so you can see the elevator on the left. I'll go this way." I pointed the opposite direction. "I'll be able to see him if he takes the one to the right." I gave Aaron a shove and started running up the sidewalk.

The elevators are in the middle of each side of the atrium oval and the glass building front faces the street. The elevators themselves are glass enclosures hanging out from the atrium walls. I figured if we each got the right angle, we should be able to cover them both and see the floor where the elevator stopped.

I got to my position but didn't see anything. I saw Aaron returning to our point of origin. I was huffing and puffing when I got back. Been skipping too many morning jogs, I thought.

Aaron said, "I saw the elevator go up, but it was damn hard to tell what floor he went to. I tried to count floors, but…damn hard to tell. Somewhere around four…I think."

Dennis walked up while we were talking. I went back over our trip inside to the guard desk, about Eberheart arriving and taking the elevator to the fourth floor, maybe. "By the way, if you'd return you voice messages and call me back, I wouldn't have to go into all this detail." I let that soak in for a moment and then added, "Can you get a search warrant?"

Dennis looked down at the sidewalk and I heard a long sigh escape. Then he said, "Let's see if I have it right. I'm going to a judge and tell him about a fictional movie character signing into the Midtown Atrium Towers Building on Saturday—and forgetting to sign out. On top of that, we have a person who works in the building come by today and maybe get off the elevator at some floor he doesn't work on. That should be convincing."

"All right," I said. "You can drop the sarcasm. Can we at least go in and see if the guard will let you in to snoop around those floors?"

"I'll go. You two stay here."

Staying outside turned out to be a good idea. While Aaron and I waited across the street, Eberheart came out of the front door. He headed down the street, around a corner and disappeared.

"I wonder if we should have followed him," I said.

"He would have seen us, and we don't know for sure whether he's done something with Effie."

"I'm pretty damn sure he has."

Dennis came out of the MAT building and we crossed the street to meet him. He wasn't able to do anything but talk to the guard. That was a waste of time. The guard wouldn't admit to knowing anything about Eberheart. "I told him I could get a warrant and search anyway. He said go ahead—that would cover his ass."

"We can't forget about Effie," I said.

"There's nothing we can do here now," Dennis said. "Go on home and Effie may still show up on her own. I've got to get some sleep; I'm beat from the night shift. I'll call you tomorrow morning. I should be back on days by then." He stood there shaking his head. "You and your crew are going to get me fired yet. Hope the three of you are prepared to support an out-of-work policeman."

Aaron and I started for home. I knew I wouldn't be able to get my mind off Effie or be able to sleep tonight—unless I heard from her.

42

MY PREDICTION OF THE DAY BEFORE WAS CORRECT. We didn't hear from Effie and I spent a sleepless night. Aaron told me it was the same for him. He also said he called his boss and let him know he would be taking a few days of vacation.

The weekend was over and today I had an excuse for being in the Midtown Atrium Towers Building. Eberheart would have a tough time keeping track of me. Aaron would drive his own car downtown in case we both needed transportation during the day.

I tried to reach Dennis during breakfast. None of his phones answered. Damn him. Where the hell is he when I need him?

"I'll be in the lobby of your building by eight-thirty. You've got my cell phone number, haven't you?" Aaron said.

I double checked my address book, verified his number and was out the door.

* * *

With the Mustang tucked into Worthington's parking slot in the basement, I walked up the stairs. I was half-way across the lobby when my cell rang. It was Dennis. I chewed him out for not answering his phone.

"If you'll stop yakking for a minute, I'll tell you what's going on." I shut up and he picked up the conversation. "I'm set up for day shifts again. I ran your fears past my boss and he agrees with me. Things sound suspicious, but there isn't enough to get a warrant. I filed a missing persons report on Effie. My boss did authorize some time for me to investigate a bit. I'm tied up for most of the day, but I can be there around three this afternoon."

"We've got to do something to find Effie before that. If you can't do it, I will."

"Casey, please don't get in over your head."

"I've got my gun."

"That's what I mean. Don't get in so deep you pull the damn weapon only to find out you won't use it."

"I'll talk to you later, Dennis." I punched the END button on my cell phone.

I whizzed through my workload in record time. I left enough paperwork on my desktop, so I could feign having something to do. I dialed Aaron's number on my cell phone at a quarter to nine. He answered and I told him the building grapevine told me there was unfinished space on two different floors. I told him to check around the third floor. "I'll be on five for a while. Did you bring the door stops with you?"

He said yes and we agreed to meet in the lobby in a half hour.

* * *

When I arrived in the lobby, Aaron was waiting. I told him I made a pass through the fifth floor and didn't find anything suspicious there.

"I didn't see anything concrete on three," he said, "but half the area is empty. It's blocked off next to the elevators, so someone could be at the far end and I wouldn't have heard anyone."

"I wonder if Dennis checked the other tower during his investigation. So far all we've looked at is this building. Do you remember Dennis saying anything about that?"

"No. I can see if there's unused space over there. How about I meet you back here around noon? We can have lunch and compare notes."

"Let's not waste too much time," I said. "Effie's been missing since Saturday. Yesterday I could fool myself into thinking she might be staying with someone. Today, I'm scared to death something's happened to her."

"I'm just as concerned. But we've got to be careful and not rush into a situation that makes everything worse."

"Let me have some of those magnetic door stops." He handed four to me. That meant with these and my name tag, I could block five doors open. That ought to be enough.

I said, "Before you head over there, make sure the access door to the utility shaft on ten is blocked open."

"Make damn sure you wait till I get back before you check out the third floor."

"Okay. Back here at noon," I said.

* * *

I passed through my cubicle and shuffled papers, shifting them from one corner of my desk to another. Next I dropped a couple of checks off in Wayne Harmon's office. I leaned over the reception counter and whispered to Cheryl. "I've got to get out of the office for a little while. I'll be in the building, but I need to know if anyone is looking for me." I handed her a slip of paper. "Here's my cell phone number. Call me if anyone asks about me."

"What's going on? You know Mr. Eberheart is mad at you?"

I frowned and shrugged like I wasn't aware.

"Yep, I heard him in Mr. Harmon's office. He said you were trouble. What did he mean?"

"I think he has an ego problem."

I made sure my cell phone ringer was set to vibrate. I picked up my purse and left the office.

On the way to the restroom—when I was sure no one from the office was in sight—I used a magnet to block the door to the stairwell. Climbing up the stairs to ten and back down the utility shaft to three didn't take as long as I thought it might. I eased the door open enough to slip a magnetic strip into the door jam. The climb to nine, up those metal rungs, was the long way around, but I didn't want to go into the third floor without a back way out.

I returned to my floor and took the elevator. The door opened on three and I looked around. The construction area door was padlocked. It was twisted to the closed position, but not locked. Aaron strikes again, I thought. He does good work.

I slid the gun out of my purse, eased the slide back and released it to put a shell in the chamber. I reholstered the gun, took a deep breath and inched the door open. It squeaked, but not loud enough for anyone inside to hear, I hoped.

43

THE SQUEAKING DOOR WAS BEHIND ME. THE
construction on this part of the floor began and stopped before
it could be finished. There was a corridor leading through the
middle with doorways on both sides. At the far end, there was
another door to what must have been the last twenty feet of
floor space.

I moved down the hallway with a slow pace, checking the
side rooms as I passed. I spotted the entrance to the utility shaft
and arrived at the final door at the end of the hall. Opening it
about two inches, I peeked through the crack at the hinge side.
I looked as far into the room as the opening permitted. Nothing
was visible so, I opened it far enough to poke my head in.

Effie was sitting in a chair in the center of the room. I could
see duct tape binding her and a strip of it over her mouth. She
spotted me as soon as my head appeared through the doorway
and shook her head violently. I was frowning, trying to understand her signal when something slammed me in the back. It
reminded me of my initial day in the building when Gene Morse
knocked me out of the way of the first falling body.

I hit the floor and rolled in time to see the man approaching
me. It was the attacker who'd come to my condo a couple of
weeks ago. I could remember the feeling as he tried to strangle
me on my bed. There wasn't a phone handy to use as a club this
time. I scuttled like a crab on my back doing my best to put some
distance between the two of us. I was losing ground. The way he
reached down for me I guessed he was going to grab me by the
shirt front and drag me to my feet. I cupped each hand slightly.

I was right about his motives. As he began tugging at my clothing, his head came within arm's reach. I slammed my hands to each side of his head so my hands covered his ears and got the desired results. I could tell the cupped hands built up pressure on his ear drums and was causing him pain. The down side was, the pain didn't seem enough to overcome his rage. He shouted, more of a scream, and jerked me to my feet.

Both his hands went to my throat. Putting my hands together at my waist, I interlocked my fingers. I drove my hands up between his arms. The V formed by my arms forced his apart, and he lost his grip on my neck.

I raced toward Effie, but he was still too close. I passed her and continued to run. She stuck out her taped legs and tripped him.

"You god-dammed bitch," he grunted at Effie as he slid on the floor causing dust around him to swirl. "When I finish with her, I'll come back for you. It'll be real slow and painful."

I was putting distance between the two of us, but I was also getting farther from the door. I moved sideways and he circled to cut me off. I kept moving until my run for the door would pass close to Effie again. "Help me again, and I'll be back," I whispered to her. She nodded.

I ran for the door, he followed and Effie took him down again. By the time he scrambled to his feet, cursing, I was down the hall and into the room, which was my backup escape route. I went through the door, pulling the magnetic strip off the jamb, and was standing on the small platform in the utility shaft when he came into the room and rattled the door. "Come out of there, you bitch," he said. He jerked on the door again.

If he had a key, he'd be using it by now. I had a minute or two to settle my nerves and decide what to do next. I made one of those bang-the-palm-of-the-hand-on-the-forehead motions. I looked at my purse and eased my hand into the holster section.

The door shook again. I was as quiet as I could be and listened for his footsteps. It sounded like he was returning to the room where Effie was being held. I can't let him get to her.

I opened the door and replaced the magnetic strip. With the door half open, I could see him standing about ten feet away. He was grinning and held a large knife in his hand.

"Come on in here, bitch. I got something for you. And when I'm through screwing you, I'll give you this."

He held the knife extended and took a step toward me. My fingers closed around the butt of the Glock and I drew it from its holster. "One more step and I'll put three in your chest." The firmness in my voice surprised me.

"I don't think you got the balls."

I remembered Dennis' warning. I moved into a two-handed shooting stance hoping it would make him believe I was serious.

44

I FELT LIKE I WAS READY TO PUKE. I GRITTED MY teeth, and firmed my grip on the pistol. Three and evaluate, I remember my weapons instructor saying. Three and evaluate—and be ready to fire three more. Count, when you've done that three times, there's only one left in the chamber—time to eject the empty magazine and slam a loaded one home.

He took the step.

I squeezed off three rounds and looked at him. He was flat on the floor on his back. There were three dark red spots in the center of his chest, and the red was spreading out to form a single stain. Evaluation—he was dead. I turned my head and heaved up my guts.

I coughed and spit the disgusting taste from my mouth, then wiped my mouth on my sleeve. Wow, that's pretty gross; I wonder if everyone feels this bad after shooting a human being—even one who is ready to kill you. Probably.

I focused my attention and moved out of the room, stopping to listen every few feet until I reached the end of the hall again. When I looked in this time, Effie was alone. I holstered the gun, got the tape off her hands and she ripped the piece from her mouth.

"I heard shots. Where's the guy who was in here?" she said.

"I shot him. He won't give anyone problems again."

"Thank God. Am I ever glad to see you," she said. She reached down and picked at the tape around her ankles. "How did you know where I was?"

I told her what Dennis, Aaron and I had been doing since she disappeared on Saturday. "Most of it was blind luck. Enough of that. What did you mean with the phone message you left me? What did you find?"

"I was up on the tenth floor looking for Mr. Eberheart's badge. I found it. It must have been a one-in-a-million shot but it's inside one of those metal wall studs lying on the floor. I guess it sailed through the air and slid into the end of one of those tubes. Like I said, one-in-a-million." She stood up and put both arms around my neck.

"Did you get it out?"

"No, it's about a foot inside the stud. I was looking for something I could use to drag it out when I thought it might be better to leave it alone. It puts Eberheart at the scene of the crime—but what if Mr. Hawkins' fingerprints are on it too? That would put Eberheart there at the time of the murder."

"That's good thinking. So it's still up there. Inside the stud?"

She nodded. "And that's when the creep you shot grabbed me. He clamped a hand over my mouth before I knew he was there. Since I was wandering around looking for a stick or something, he didn't know where I'd been or what I'd found. He kept asking, but I told him I didn't find anything."

She rubbed her wrists where the tape residue was still visible. Effie looked beat, so I told her to sit down and rest for a minute. She wasn't sure she wanted to use the chair where she was held captive, but she sank into it anyway.

"I need to get word to Aaron and Dennis," I said. "Dennis is on his way down here and Aaron is checking out the other MAT tower."

Effie doubled over and said, "I need a potty break—bad."

"You can use the one on this floor; don't worry about it not being connected to plumbing." I found a small package of tissues in an outside pocket of my purse and handed them to her.

Effie re-appeared with a smile on her face. I put my hand down into my purse feeling for my cell phone and was having major trouble locating it. I was about to dump the whole damn thing upside down to ease the search. Effie looked up at me and her mouth dropped open.

"Effie, what's wrong?"

"Behind you," she said.

45

EBERHEART WAS ADVANCING TOWARD ME. HIS VOICE was shrill. "How the hell did you get down here, Fremont? Who the hell shot Newman?"

"Who's Newman?" I said, hoping he would take the time to respond to my question. I reached for Effie's hand and jerked her to her feet. I turned my back on Eberheart and whispered, "Follow me—we're going straight through him."

Eberheart was more than a medium build, but I was banking on the element of surprise. I was still holding her hand as I charged toward the man blocking our exit from the room. I lowered my shoulder and hit him full in the chest—a bit off center. Either we were good or we were lucky. I didn't care which. Eberheart spun around, tripped over his own feet and went to the floor.

I felt Effie jerk to a half stop as we passed the body of the man I shot, the man whose name was Newman according to Eberheart. "Don't stop now. Get through there." Like my last trip into the shaft, I retrieved my magnet and slammed the door. "Get up the ladder. We're going to the tenth floor."

I knew if Eberheart was carrying his key to the shaft doors, he wouldn't be far behind. While he was getting his key out, we could get a head start on him. I didn't figure on Effie's lack of stamina. A couple of days as a prisoner, tied up most of the time, took their toll. She was climbing in slow motion. I urged her to move faster, but she seemed to be going full tilt for the physical condition she was in after being held captive.

I heard the door below me open and I saw Eberheart poke his head through. He looked down, then up and spotted us. We had about a two-floor head start, but he was closing the gap. Effie approached the eighth floor and I told her to go for the platform and open the door.

"Where will that lead?" she said.

"Beats the hell out of me, but it's better than getting trapped here in the shaft."

Effie did what I told her and disappeared into—somewhere on eight. As I stepped onto the platform, a hand grabbed my ankle. The tug dropped me onto my butt on the concrete slab. I saw Eberheart's face appear over the edge and I lashed out with a foot. The kick was aimed at his skull and glanced off his forehead. It gave me enough time to roll through the door and slam it shut.

"Damn," I said. "This is the Boneventure Accounting office."

There was a four-drawer file cabinet sitting next to the door. I waved at Effie and we tipped the file over. Lying on the floor, it blocked Eberheart's way in. A female office worker looked at us with eyes wide. "Excuse the mess," I told her.

I gave Effie a head nod and we walked out of the office acting as casual as we could. "Let's go down to the garage and get out of here," I said.

"Do you think the elevator is safe? Maybe we should take the stairs. I don't want to run into that guy again. Who was he anyway?"

I forgot Effie heard Eberheart's name before, but never saw him until today. "That was Eberheart. No telling which way he went—up or down. And no way telling where he is now. Let's take a couple of minutes to see if I can get a call through to Dennis or Aaron." I dialed them both and neither answered.

I did a mental coin toss. "Let's take the stairs to the lobby and then to the garage."

As I bounced down the stairs, I thought of trying to call 9-1-1. I fumbled the phone out of my purse and punched the numbers with trembling fingers. All I got was a loud screeching sound.

Looking at my phone I could see I dialed 9-2-2. Try again Casey. When I got the same sound and saw another misdialed attempt, I shoved the phone back into my purse. I don't have time for this.

I was keeping a watchful eye over my shoulder as Effie opened the door to the parking garage. We stepped through, and I closed the door.

She said, "Guess we went the wrong direction."

46

EBERHEART WAS STANDING IN FRONT OF US IN THE garage. How the hell did he get down here so fast, I asked myself. Avenues of escape raced through my mind: dash for the Mustang—back up the stairway—about then I ran out of ideas. The only other alternative was to stay here and confront him. The two of us defeated him before. Perhaps defeat was too strong a word. He didn't brandish a weapon earlier. Of course, he could have something concealed that still wasn't visible.

He took the decision away from us. Eberheart was advancing and he had a gun in his hand. I wondered if I could draw my own pistol before he could pull the trigger. No way. That's ludicrous, Casey, I told myself. I'd have to be faster than a speeding bullet, and that fast I ain't.

"Get into the stairway," he said. "We're going back up to the third floor. I still need to know what you two have been up to…"

I turned around and pulled the door open. Effie and I stepped through. Eberheart ordered us to stop, and he asked me where the gun was.

"What gun?"

"Don't play stupid, or think I am. The gun you used to kill Newman, bitch."

Now I was really pissed. I'd rather he called me by my last name than the term he used. If I get the chance, asshole, I'll drop you like a bad habit. "I dropped it somewhere in the utility shaft. I heard it clatter clear to the bottom."

"Put your hands behind your head and interlace your fingers."

Effie and I both complied. Eberheart reached under my arm and put a hand into my purse. I felt him rummaging around inside and could feel the muzzle of his gun in my back. He didn't notice the separate holster section of the handbag, but he did locate my cell phone.

"Where the hell was that?" I said. "I was trying to find it earlier." I hoped this dodge would interrupt his search efforts. If I'm lucky he'll overlook the gun.

"Shut up. Get moving up the stairs." He shoved the gun harder into my back. "If you try anything going through the lobby, I put a bullet in this other lady's back…then I'll take care of you on the spot."

We crossed the lobby from the garage stairs to the stairwell leading to the upper floors. I couldn't believe the timing, Aaron was coming toward us. I hoped Eberheart wouldn't recognize him. I devised several signals on the spot. Mind's still working, eh Casey, I told myself. When I was sure Aaron was looking at me I moved my head from side to side in a slow, deliberate manner. I formed the words "not now" with my mouth and prayed he was a lip reader.

Eberheart gave me several sharp jabs in the back with his gun. I realized I'd slowed down staring at Aaron. Next I extended three fingers and brought the hand up to my chin and mouthed "third floor." Aaron squinted at the signal and I said another short prayer. Next I made a circle of the fingers and thumb of my left hand—a bit like a telescope—except the "hole" was vertical. I put both hands in front of me where Eberheart couldn't see them. I brought the index finger of my right hand up through the hole of my left hand. Aaron frowned again and looked at my face—I mouthed the word "shaft." If he didn't get the inference, the hand signal could take on an image of a rather gross gesture referring to intercourse. My last effort at communicating was to ask Aaron to get in touch with Dennis. I couldn't think of any hand signals to convey that one, so I formed the words "call Dennis" twice.

We reached the doorway to the stairs and I saw Aaron turn away. Did I see a look of acknowledgement or one of absolute confusion? I couldn't decide, but I knew he was smart and could work it out. I preferred the optimistic spin, because the alternative left us alone to face whatever Eberheart was planning.

"Why are you so interested in what we were doing up on the tenth floor?" I asked Eberheart.

"I want to know what you know. Did you find anything up there?"

I kept my mouth shut. The silence was too much for him.

"I want to be sure there's nothing up there to incriminate me."

I said, "Incriminate?"

"Yeah. That Hawkins was going to blow the whistle on us, so I threw the son-of-a-bitch over the railing."

I guess he's confident neither of us would testify against him. That meant we wouldn't survive the day. Hell, we might not survive the next ten minutes.

Since he seemed to be in a talkative mood, I decided to press further. "Who else was working with you? Who killed Mr. Worthington?"

The gun poked me hard in the spine. The conversation seemed over.

At the door to the third floor, I took the handle and shook it back and forth. "Looks like the door is locked."

"Bullshit, Fremont," he said. "I know about your magnets. I discovered that trick the other day. Open the freaking door."

I pushed through and the three of us entered the unoccupied space near the elevator. My mind was racing, but I was having trouble formulating a plan. I expended all my adrenaline earlier.

Eberheart said, "Okay, now you both tell me everything you know."

Effie and I both shook our heads. She said, "I'll never tell you anything. Even if you hurt me."

"That's sweet, Lady. How about I start hurting your friend here." He waved the gun in my direction.

I saw Effie's face go pale.

47

IT WAS AS THOUGH WE READ EACH OTHER'S MINDS. Effie and I moved apart. We did it in slow motion and I hoped Eberheart wasn't paying attention to what we were up to. I also noticed I was hoping a lot this morning. I needed more of a plan—wishful thinking only goes so far.

"Stand still," he said.

We took that as a signal to take a giant step apart, putting about five feet between us. Not enough to make a hell of a lot of difference. I shrugged and the purse strap slipped off my shoulder. I caught the strap in my right hand.

Eberheart frowned at me like he was trying to read my mind. I hoped he couldn't. There goes the hoping again. I put my head down to my chest and looked at Effie. I raised my head in one quick movement. Effie did some mind reading and took two steps away from me. That riveted Eberheart's full attention on her.

I swung my purse one full revolution over my head and aimed at his noggin. Damn good aim, I thought. I took a step forward and the handbag, weighted by the Glock, caught him square on the side of the head. He went down like a sack of rocks.

"Get out of here," I shouted to Effie. I directed her into the room where Newman's body still lay. Aaron came through the door from the shaft. I heard Eberheart pounding down the hall and I scrabbled for my gun.

I was pointing the Glock at the doorway when Eberheart entered. "Drop it, asshole," I shouted. "Look down and you can see the results of the last person in this room who disregarded my order."

He didn't pay any more attention than Newman. He was bringing his gun up to bear on me. Aaron launched himself at Eberheart. I knew he would be too late. The distance to travel was too far. The distraction was enough, though.

I shouted one last warning at Eberheart and squeezed the trigger three times. He spun around and went down on his face. Like Newman, I was damn sure he was dead too. Repeating my earlier performance, I bent over and experienced a case of the dry heaves.

I heard a cell phone buzzing, looked around the room, and realized it was my phone in Eberheart's pocket. Dennis was on the other end. "You're a day late and a dollar short, Detective," I told him. "We're on the third floor and there are two dead bodies. Best get your buns up here."

48

AARON, EFFIE AND I WERE SO CRANKED, DENNIS couldn't make sense of any of it. "You two shut up," he said pointing at my cohorts. "You," his finger swung around to me, "run the case for me."

I went over Effie's part first. How she discovered the ID badge on ten, and what we guessed happened. "If Hawkins' prints are on the badge, we know Eberheart was on the tenth floor when Hawkins went over the rail."

"That still doesn't tie him to the second murder. Put that aside for the moment. Go over the rest of the story and how you happened to kill two people."

I told him about the chase around the building and Newman coming at me with a knife.

"Ain't that just like a dumb criminal," Dennis said. "Bringing a knife to a gun fight."

I said, "I saw that movie too." I covered the balance of the chase, and this time I had two witnesses to Eberheart's shooting.

Effie and Aaron both jumped in and confirmed my story. Aaron started, "If Casey hadn't stopped him—"

"He would have killed all of us," Effie finished.

I added, "Even if we don't find the fingerprints on the ID badge, we have his confession. Two witnesses will hold up... won't they?"

Dennis confirmed my assumption. During the discussions, we worked our way down to the lobby and tried to relax over coffee. "Might as well pack up your personal things, Casey. I think your working days at Cyber-Technology are over," Dennis said.

I shook my head. "Why?"

"I think the fraud accusations will shut them down. And, we've still got the second murder to solve."

Effie jumped in. "We think Mr. Eberheart did it. We think the two killings are tied to one another."

Aaron and I were both nodding in agreement.

Dennis said, "That may well be true, but I don't have any definitive evidence proving your theory. Between us, I think you are right, but the District Attorney's office is picky—they tend to like a little proof. I think the investigation will shut C-T down at least for the time being."

"Well, hell," I said. "Effie, come on along with me. I'll gather up my meager belongings and fill out a time card. I can get Mr. Harmon to sign it before I leave."

49

"MR. HARMON, I NEED TO TAKE THE REST OF THE week off," I said.

He looked at me. "What the hell am I supposed to do to replace you?"

"If you get into a real bind, you can call the TrueTemp agency. I'm heading to my work station. I'll complete a time card and you can sign it."

By the look on his face, he wasn't the least bit happy, but I didn't wait for any further objections. I took Effie by the arm and led her to my cubicle. She was gawking as we walked. "I haven't seen this part of the office before."

I realized that when the three of us broke into Harmon's office, we were in and out. She hadn't seen the area where I worked. I said "Hi" to Cheryl and introduced Effie as we headed toward the back of the office.

* * *

"That's about it," I said and lifted the half-filled box. "Let's get out of here. We can contact your employer, make excuses and take a well deserved break."

Effie stepped close to me, reached over the box and wrapped her arms around me. We embraced each other and I think the tears in our eyes were from relief. "You're right," she said. "Let's go home."

"Where the hell do you think you're going?"

Wayne Harmon was standing outside my cubicle. There was a gun in his hand. There wasn't a drop of adrenaline left, and I was damned tired of people pointing guns and knives at me. I felt like I was going to sag to the floor. I was right. I dropped the box and drooped to the floor. I could hear Effie shouting at me.

I was conscious enough to see and hear what was happening. She reached for my purse, swung it around over her head and advanced toward Harmon.

"You stupid bitch." He ducked under the arc of the purse and back-handed Effie. She staggered but kept swinging the purse. A large red welt appeared on her cheek.

"We were riding a sweet gig here until the two of you spoiled it all. I know what happened to Eberheart. Cheryl heard the rumors and told me."

"Effie, leave him alone," I said. It was more of a croak than a voice.

She didn't pay much attention. The speed of the swinging purse slowed for a moment, then she resumed the original velocity. Harmon kept ducking and swiping at her. He caught her in the face again. This time she went down, and she tossed the purse toward me as she fell.

Harmon advanced toward her, the gun trained at her head. I regained some of my composure and struggled to pull my gun from its holster.

"Why are you so concerned about us?" I asked Harmon.

"I guess you got a confession out of Eberheart. It's a matter of time until you tie me to Worthington's death."

I couldn't believe my ears. We figured Eberheart as the real boss and the man responsible for both murders. "You mean you killed him?"

"Yes, and now I have to kill the both of you if I have any chance of getting away."

I drew my Glock out and was pointing it at him, but was at a disadvantage. I was still on the floor and didn't have much maneuvering room. I threatened him. Effie did the same. We kept up the chatter, because each time we did he swung his gun toward the last person to speak.

The Mexican standoff couldn't last long. I was getting desperate. The thought of heaving my guts out for the third time was weighing me down. I didn't think I could do it. The one thing that kept me going was when he pointed his gun at Effie. I couldn't bear the thought of her being shot.

My own personal detective came riding to our rescue. I heard Dennis shout, "Police, don't turn around. Drop the gun. Drop the gun or I will fire."

Harmon decided he would prefer going to jail rather than die on the spot. That was my guess when he put his weapon down on a nearby desk. After all, there were two pistols trained on him—front and back. No way he could survive a shootout. Then it hit me. Even if Harmon died, he might have shot one of us—maybe even Effie. I rolled onto my side and puked again. "Son-of-a-bitch," I said. "I didn't even shoot anyone this time."

I gave Dennis and another police officer who arrived on the scene in C-T's offices on nine a quick run-down on Effie then returned with her to the lobby. We got off the elevator and Aaron looked worried as he hurried toward us.

With a furrowed brow, he said, "When Dennis took off he told me to stay put. You okay?"

We both nodded and Effie took the lead. She described what happened at Cyber-Technology.

"Were we right about what happened?" he said.

I said, "I think we were close, but I didn't get all the details. We know who killed who, but we don't know why it happened."

Aaron pointed behind me. When I turned, I saw Dennis step out of an elevator. Two policemen were leading a handcuffed Wayne Harmon toward the front door. Dennis veered off and approached the three of us. We all spoke at once, asking him what he knew.

"Calm down," Dennis said. Standing in the middle of the lobby, he related what transpired after Effie and I left the ninth floor. "Harmon starting talking despite the Miranda warning I gave him. He may be trying to lay off the details, so he'll look innocent of the murders—"

I jumped in. "He can't deny the Worthington killing. Effie and I can testify he admitted to that one." Effie gave an emphatic nod.

Dennis continued, "Okay. We probably have him on the Worthington killing."

"Don't forget, Eberheart admitted to the first murder, too," I said. "Effie and I heard him admit to it. Did he say anything about why it all happened?"

Dennis picked up the story. "He yakked non-stop all the way down on the elevator …"

Effie, Aaron and I crowded even closer to Dennis. He tried to push clear, but we weren't budging.

"According to Harmon," Dennis said, "Hawkins learned about the fraud CT was involved in and threatened to go to the police. Eberheart tried to warn him off, but Hawkins persisted. Eberheart lured him up to the tenth floor and pushed him over the railing. Hawkins' shoe came off in the scuffle and Eberheart kicked it under the railing. Also during the struggle, Hawkins ripped the ID tag off Eberheart. The ID itself ended up where Effie found it and Hawkins was still clutching the chain when he fell to his death."

"Why was Ross Worthington killed?" I said.

"He was willing to go along with the fraud," Dennis said, "but he was getting panicky about the killing. Eberheart tried to warn him off, but he wouldn't listen and was ready to give himself up. This is where the stories diverge. Eberheart told you he killed Hawkins, but he didn't say anything about Worthington. Now Harmon claims Eberheart did the second one too."

Effie and I started to jump in, but Dennis held up his hand and said, "I know, you both heard Harmon admit to the second killing. Whoever did the second one, it's pretty obvious it was to get rid of a potential stoolie. Actually, I guess that was the reason for both killings. Hawkins was ready to tell the police about the fraud at C-T and Worthington was going to blow the whistle on his cohorts at Cyber-Technology."

* * *

It was late afternoon before all the questioning was over, before the crime scene investigators finished their work on the third floor and in the Cyber-Technology offices.

It dawned on me at last that I didn't know what brought Dennis up to C-T in the nick of time. He told us Cheryl, the Cyber-Technology receptionist warned him. Earlier she told Harmon what she heard about Eberheart—when she saw him follow us back to my desk, she beat it down to the lobby and found Dennis.

That, as they say, was that.

I looked down at the cold dregs of the coffee in my third or fourth, or was it my fifth, cup of coffee. Dennis looked at me and I asked him when we could get out of the MAT building and added, "I've seen more of this place than I want to."

Aaron and Effie nodded in agreement. I fumbled inside my purse and pulled out my time card. "Damn," I said. "I forgot to have Harmon sign this thing. I guess I can miss one day's pay. Let's get out of here."

Dennis said, "I think we can let you go now. If anyone wants you…" He waved an arm around at the numerous police officers still milling about the lobby, "we know where to find you."

"Dennis, how about you coming over for dinner tonight?" I said.

Effie and Aaron stumbled all over one another's words indicating they could find some other place to spend the night. I smiled at their efforts.

"I appreciate the offers," I said, "but I think Dennis deserves a decent meal, and you know he won't get it if left to my devices."

"Is this an invitation to whatever occurs after dinner as well?" Dennis said.

"You never know," I said. "You never know." I hoped the look on my face conveyed my feelings.

The four musketeers linked arms and marched out of the MAT building.

THE END

ABOUT THE AUTHOR

John Achor's writing assignments have appeared in a variety of local, national and international publications such as Good Old Days, Computer Pilot, The Storyteller and Writers' Journal. He enjoys writing about, "The subjects I know best: the military, flying and people I've known." After that, John says he lets a vivid imagination take over.

The first of his three careers spanned twenty years as a U.S. Air Force pilot. He accumulated over 4,000 hours flying planes from Piper Cubs to the military equivalent of the Boeing 707.

After the military, he entered the real estate industry. He joined a national real estate franchise as a management consultant working at the regional and national levels. Those positions led him to Phoenix, Arizona, and an affiliation with a major Savings & Loan institution.

In John's words, "When the Savings and Loan industry melted away like a lump of sugar in hot coffee, I knew it was time to develop a third career." He became a freelance computer instructor, user-developer, consultant, writer and Community College instructor.

In the 1990s, John began developing characters to fill ideas he had in mind for thrillers and mystery novels. The thriller series features Alex Hilliard, and Air Force pilot, and a thirty-something lady is the leading light in the Casey Fremont mystery series.

By the 2000s, he put five novels featuring Casey Fremont and Alex Hilliard in the can and launched his writing career. He and his wife left Arizona for Arkansas and later relocated to Nebraska. From there, John continues writing and has ideas in mind for a third thriller and has completed the first chapters of the fourth mystery novel.

WHAT'S COMING DOWN THE ROAD...

Author John Achor's amateur female detective returns ready to tackle crime once more and along with her side-kicks become involved in her second adventure *Three, Four – Kill Some More*.

Casey Fremont's ex-husband, Jarvis the Rat, is two months behind with alimony payments, so she asks the TrueTemp Agency to find a temp job for her—this time with a legal firm. Casey's life with her two roommates and detective boyfriend continues as the new job begins. At the same time, postcards start arriving in her mailbox. They contain images and cryptic messages—messages Casey believes relate to a series of murders occurring in the local area.

Needing to decipher the messages to prevent further deaths, Casey has to battle both her stalker, the mysterious and deadly "Romeo," and convince the police they are on the wrong trail. She realizes failure to solve the mystery may be fatal to her and her friends.

ADDED BONUS MATERIAL,
A SHORT STORY BY JOHN ACHOR

Author's note:
The Hemingway-Pfeiffer Museum and Education Center,
the Downtown Inn and Piggott, Arkansas do exist;
however this is a work of pure fiction.

MURDER AT THE DOWNTOWN INN

A CASEY FREMONT MYSTERY SHORT STORY

THE ACCOUNTANT SLOWED HIS CAR AND EASED IT to the wrong side of the narrow road. The smell of newly resurfaced asphalt assaulted his nostrils when he rolled down a window. He braked as the mailbox with an upraised red flag was opposite him. A glance down the road and in the rearview mirror confirmed no one in sight. Metal squeaked against metal as he opened the door of the box and pulled envelopes out. A pair addressed to Piggott, Arkansas caught his eye. He planned to open, read and reseal the letters, then place them in a letter drop later in the day. The rest went back into the mailbox.

At home, he passed the envelopes through the steam produced by the whistling tea kettle. While he waited for the vapor to do its job, he looked around his home. It was a drab two-room efficiency apartment devoid of any human input in the way of decor. He no longer could call himself a CPA, reducing him to taking menial jobs.

The letter contents seemed out of character for her, but a couple of hundred miles from home would finally offer him an opportunity. It would be a good place to get even with this person who got him fired all those years ago. He jotted down names and phone numbers and reglued the envelope flaps. Within an hour, he added his own reservations at a bed and breakfast and a weeklong writers' retreat to the stack and entrusted them to the USPS. The swinging door to the letter box clanged shut. He smiled.

* * *

Casey Fremont kicked her red Mustang up to sixty-five and enjoyed the wind whooshing around the windshield. She hoped to keep the top down for the entire trip to Piggott. Eastbound on I-630, she and Effie Tremayne reviewed the route to this small Arkansas town—about as far north and east as you can go and remain in the state.

The brochure suggested the Hemingway-Pfeiffer Museum and Learning Center in Piggott as a great place to learn about writing. Casey loved reading mysteries, but now she anticipated a full week retreat devoted to putting words on paper. Her finances were in decent shape. Casey's ex, Jarvis the Rat, sent this month's tribute—she preferred to think of it as payment due for all his screwing around—on time for a change. Her accommodations were prepaid at a bed and breakfast inn, with lunches included in the seminar fee and there was enough cash in her purse for incidentals.

Heading out of Little Rock, Casey picked up U. S. 67-167 going northeast. The divided portion gave way to two-lane as the tires hummed along the roadway. Scenery varied—from flat and straight to the curving road and hills of the Crowley's Ridge area.

In Piggott, Effie and Casey missed the Downtown Inn the first time by. A trip around the town square gave them a better perspective and Casey eased the Mustang into an open parking slot near the front door. Inside, Casey eyed the stairs. It was a straight shot to the second floor, but like many old, remodeled buildings there were more than two dozen steps. Midway up, was a landing. Overloaded, Casey paused at the halfway point and rested for a moment on the bench sitting along the wall. It took Casey two trips to lug all her gear into the building. Sarah, the innkeeper, greeted them on their first excursion up the flight of stairs. She gave them a quick tour and said coffee would be brewing by six a.m. Breakfast was available at seven-thirty. Wow, two catered meals a day. Casey decided she was going to enjoy the leisure—and probably gain a pound or two.

* * *

On his way to Piggott, the Accountant stopped for a meal and rescued a second-hand copy of a national newspaper from a trash can. The paper's cover story was about workplace murders.

He could sympathize with the killers. After all, their provocations were like his, but he didn't kill anyone—yet. Those co-workers and managers got what they deserved, he thought. He noted evenly divided outcomes. Half the assailants were captured and sentenced to death or life in prison while the remainder killed themselves or were shot by the police. The Accountant thought, none of those scenarios are acceptable. I won't kill myself and I'm too smart to get caught. When I finish this chore, I may just go back to the accounting firm and take out a few more. His "chore" this week was to kill the person responsible for his current sad situation.

* * *

Monday morning was overcast. The smells coming from Sarah's kitchen drew Casey down the second floor hall to the dining area. She ate more breakfast than usual and then headed west to cover the five blocks or so to the Hemingway Educational Center. She climbed out, and Effie took the car for the day.

The variety of the people attending this retreat amazed Casey—age, gender, background, experience—and all with a common interest in writing. The facilitator, Dr. Larry, led the early morning group warm-up session. He was kinda hunky and didn't wear a ring on his left hand. Casey wondered…She avoided eye contact because she figured it was better to concentrate on other aspects of the retreat.

Afterwards, individuals continued the day working on their own. Some created prose or poetry while others edited previous efforts. Casey found inspiration everywhere and from everyone. She opted to use her laptop in the Barn Studio where Hemingway wrote in the 1930s.

* * *

The first night, the Accountant spent the evening reading in the upper hall ticking off the roomers in his mind. There was only one left who was not in their room. He not only switched the lights off, but also loosened the bulbs. Now the Accountant waited on the darkened stairway of the Downtown Inn. Seated on the bench halfway up the straight staircase and dressed in black, he was not visible in the shadows. When the last of the writers, Faith, came up the stairs, a well-placed foot sent her sprawling back down the thirteen steps to the bottom. A low gasp escaped from Faith's mouth when she hit the foot of the stairs. The Accountant hurried down and injected potassium into a vein in her arm knowing the reaction would be ventricular fibrillation followed by cardiac arrest. He doubted the local coroner would look further and conclude: death by infarction, bruises accumulated in the fall down the stairs during the heart attack. Satisfied, the Accountant made his way to his own room upstairs tightening the bulbs in their sockets as he went.

* * *

On Tuesday morning, Casey and Effie were greeted by all the other roomers and the local police. They found it difficult to eat the scrambled egg and sausage casserole Sarah prepared before she found Faith at the bottom of the stairway.

At the Learning Center, the group session was taken over by a discussion of the death of one of their own. Al, an older man with a gray beard said, "I figured if anyone would get dizzy and fall down a flight of stairs, it would be me."

Jordan, another Little Rock area resident, said with a wink, "Anyone else have medical problems we should keep an eye on?" Again, more smiles from those in the group.

* * *

All but one were busy with lunch preparations. The Accountant slipped the old newspaper he picked up on his way to Piggott onto the conference table. As the group ate, Bruce browsed the paper and described the feature story. Several of the writers told of witnessing employee firings, which could have led to mayhem.

"You don't suppose something like that was the motive for Faith's death, do you?" Bruce said.

Jordan said, "Of course not, she had a heart attack."

Dottie, an aspiring writer from the north side of Little Rock said, "I once turned in a guy named Littleton for embezzlement and he got the ax." She looked around the table at the men. "I guess I'm safe. None of you guys look like him."

Everyone did their best to resume a reasonable writing schedule for the balance of the day.

Effie arrived at three-thirty to pick up Casey. She joined in the conversation saying, "The local police said Faith died of natural causes."

Casey started to ask how she learned that. Then she shrugged and accepted the fact Effie could find out darn near anything from anybody. She introduced Effie to the group. Most were packing up to head back to town, but Ted announced he was going to spend another hour writing in the Barn Studio.

Effie asked Ted what the barn was and he explained it was a spot Hemingway used when he wanted to get away from the main house and write. Effie was interested, so she and Casey followed Ted. Effie took her time looking at the memorabilia and photos on the wall. Her curiosity satisfied, Effie said it was time to get back to town.

* * *

At five o'clock, Casey and Effie left the Downtown Inn for supper. They walked along the town square past the police station and crossed the street to a second side of the square. Several doors down, they came to a diner. Casey pulled the door open and the aromas of home cooking enveloped them and drew the two through the entryway.

In the middle of their meal, a buzz rippled through the dining room. Casey waved the waitress over and said, "What's going on?"

"Another one of those writers is dead. Found him out there in the barn at the Hemingway Museum."

"My God," Casey said. "This is turning into Agatha Christy's 'Ten Little Indians.' "

"Except there are…er, were…eleven of you," Effie said.

Looking at the waitress, Casey said, "Was it a guy named Ted?"

"I think it was," the waitress said.

"We should have stayed there with Ted," Effie said. "Maybe he wouldn't be dead now."

"If someone was determined to kill him, staying there would only have delayed the inevitable. Don't beat yourself up over a what-if."

"Tell me everything about your group," Effie said looking at Casey.

Casey went over all the details she could remember, starting with yesterday morning. She mentioned Dottie's comment today about getting a man fired. "She looked at each of the guys at the table: Al, Mike, Bruce, Ted, Chuck and even Dr. Larry. Then she said something like: I'm safe. None of you look like him."

"How about the other man in the group?" Effie said.

Casey wracked her brain but couldn't come up with another male—writer or mentor. They held a whispered conversation. Casey said, "Either there's a serial nut on the loose, or…we have one or more red herrings."

"What if both killings were meant to lead us astray? What if Dottie is the real intended victim?"

They finished their meal and hurried back to the corner. Crossing the street, they entered the police station. Casey told the sergeant about their suspicions. He seemed reluctant to accept their explanation saying both deaths were of natural causes. "Our coroner says they both look like heart attacks," he said.

"When was the last time you had two heart attacks in two days here in Piggott?" Effie said.

The policeman's silence told them he didn't have an answer. They both pursued the issue, but he sat there with a Mt. Rushmore expression.

Casey said, "Would you at least do me a favor?" Without waiting for his answer she continued, "Please be at the Hemingway Learning Center around nine-thirty tomorrow morning." He didn't appear happy about having his day dictated to him but agreed to the request.

* * *

The next morning, Effie and Casey dawdled in their room after breakfast. Casey made a call on her cell and told the other party what she was looking for. She finished with, "Call back by nine." The two watched the street as the writers left the Downtown Inn for the day. When they saw her leave, they allowed another ten minutes to be sure she wouldn't return. Then they slipped down the hall where Casey applied one of the skills taught her by a less-than-wholesome friend and smiled as the lock she was picking clicked open. Rummaging around the room, they located three items that would help prove their theory.

* * *

They left the Inn. Effie walked toward the police station and Casey climbed into her car. On her way to the Hemingway Museum, Casey answered her phone. Inside the Learning Center, Casey looked at her watch, which read nine-thirty, and said, "My apologies to the group. I couldn't decide what to wear today." That brought eye rolls from the males while the ladies nodded in understanding. Casey could see a police car pulling up outside, so she stalled for a couple more minutes.

Effie and the police sergeant entered and Casey said, "I asked the officer to be present today." She moved to the head of the table. When all eyes in the room were on her, she began a slow, deliberate presentation. "My friend," she said pointing at Effie, "and I did a bit of snooping—here and back in Little Rock."

Someone at the table said, "You didn't have time to get to Little Rock and back."

Casey ignored the interruption. "We, Effie and I, came to the conclusion someone in this group killed Faith and Ted. Dottie, we also suspect you are the intended victim."

Dottie seemed to shrink in her seat and edged her chair back from the table.

Casey continued, "Remember Dottie told us about getting a man fired years ago. He's the one who killed Ted and Faith to throw everyone off the track, and he's sitting here right now."

Now all the men were drawing away like Dottie did a moment ago.

"Not you guys," Casey said. "There's another man at the table." More furrowed brows and sideway glances. "Jordan, stand up," Casey said.

The lady didn't stir. She looked away. Casey leaned toward her and repeated the order. This time Jordan rose without protest. Casey said, "I have to give credit to Effie for this one. Notice Jordan's elbows are above her waist—that's male physiology. Ladies, take a look at yourselves and you can confirm your elbows are at your waistline."

Jordan pointed a finger at Casey. "You're accusing me of being a man and because of that I killed two people?" Her voice rose about a full octave during the statement. "How do we know what you say about elbows is one-hundred percent true?" By now, Jordan was near enough to wag a finger under Casey's nose. The policeman moved up behind Jordan without a sound.

Casey said, "Covering up another male trait, an Adam's apple, is probably the reason you always wear a turtleneck top. Even if I'm not correct about physiology, we found items in your room. And my contact in Little Rock confirmed some facts." She stepped aside and looked at Dottie. "What was the name of the man who was fired and when was it?"

"His name was James Littleton…and it was five years ago."

Casey turned her attention back to Jordan. "My contact in Little Rock says Littleton's history ends five years ago and there's no record of a Jordan Small before that."

"That's bull," Jordan said. Her voice dropped back to its normal range. "Nothing but a coincidence."

"Well, this isn't coincidence," Casey said. "Effie, show the folks what we found in Jordan's room this morning."

Effie stepped to the table and with a flourish worthy of a magician, lifted a Hemingway-Pfeiffer book bag onto the table.

"You didn't have my permission to go into my room. Whatever is in the bag is inadmissible as evidence," Jordan said.

Casey smiled. "I wasn't acting as an agent of the police, I'm a civilian, and I was on my own. You can accuse me of criminal trespass if you like, but a judge will be happy to accept everything in this bag."

"Even so," Jordan said with a dismissive wave, "what could you have found there?"

Casey pointed toward Effie and said, "Carry on."

Effie took over and Jordan's attention was riveted on her. "First a disposable razor," Effie said as she pulled it from the bag. "By itself, it doesn't prove much. But, most of us gals only shave our legs every few days and you wear slacks most of the time. So, how come we found a half-dozen used razors in your bag? My hunch is that you have a heavy beard and need to shave twice a day and having the used ones show up in the trash would give you away."

"More bull," Jordan said, her voice dropping to an even lower register. "Doesn't prove a thing." She took a backhanded swipe at Effie.

Effie ducked and blocked the blow. Next, she produced a small bottle from the bag. "This potassium is damning. A little research and we learned that when injected as an overdose, it causes a heart attack. The local coroner is going over the bodies again—this time with a magnifying glass looking for injection sites. Also, Casey remembers you saying on your first morning here that Faith died of a heart attack. That fact wasn't confirmed until later in the day."

Jordan seemed frozen in place, her eyes darting around the room.

Effie said, "And, then there's this item." She looked at Casey and gave an almost imperceptible nod. As Effie jerked a wig from the bag, Casey ripped another wig from Jordan's head.

"My, God," Dottie said. "That's Jim Littleton." She scrambled to her feet and stumbled backward dumping her chair over with a thud. Dottie retreated to a corner and Jordan started to follow. He, Jordan, pulled a hypodermic needle from his pocket and tore the needle cover off. Holding it above shoulder height, like a knife, he lunged at Dottie.

The police officer swung his nightstick in a wide arc. The well aimed blow caught Jordan's wrist and there was a crack as bones broke. The needle flew across the room hitting nothing but a wall. Jordan crumpled to the floor and was in handcuffs before he could scream in pain.

"I guess that ends the Case of Too Many Heart Attacks," Effie said dusting her hands against each other. "Looks like the Hemingway Museum and the Downtown Inn are safe for writers again."

THE END

www.ingramcontent.com/pod-product-compliance
Lightning Source LLC
Chambersburg PA
CBHW022046240626
47154CB00007B/2582